W9-AZE-813

NIGHT OF THE SPADEFOOT TOADS

Bill Harley

PEACHTREE
ATLANTA

Ω
Published by
PEACHTREE PUBLISHERS
1700 Chattahoochee Avenue
Atlanta, Georgia 30318-2112

www.peachtree-online.com

Jacket design by Loraine M. Joyner
Book design by Melanie McMahon Ives

Printed in November 2010 by Lake Book Manufacturing in Melrose Park, Illinois, in the United States of America
10 9 8 7 6 5 4 3 2

Library of Congress Cataloging-in-Publication Data

Harley, Bill, 1954-
Night of the spadefoot toads / Bill Harley. -- 1st ed.
p. cm.
Summary: When his family moves from Tucson, Arizona to Massachusetts, fifth-grader Ben has a hard time leaving the desert he loves, but when he finds a kindred spirit in his science teacher and ends up trying to help her with some of her problems, he finally begins to feel at home.
ISBN 13: 978-1-56145-459-4 / ISBN 10: 1-56145-459-1
[1. Moving, Household--Fiction. 2. Vernal pool ecology--Fiction. 3. Environmental protection--Fiction. 4. Teacher-student relationships--Fiction. 5. Schools--Fiction. 6. Massachusetts--Fiction.] I. Title.
PZ7.H22655Ni 2008
[Fic]--dc22

2008008784

This book is dedicated to all teachers of science who instill a sense of wonder for the natural world in their students. In particular, to my friends Suzy Williams, Rob "Otter" Brown, Suzanne Elliot, and most especially Carol Entin, who showed me the spadefoots close to my home on a very rainy April night.

Thanks to Suzy Williams, Suzanne Elliot, and Carol Entin for their careful reading; to Beth Samuels, who read an early version; to Tom Tyning for his comments on the manuscript and advice on timber rattlers; to Brad Fiero for advice on the natural history of the Sonoran desert; and to editors Emily Whitten and Vicky Holifield for their care and wisdom. And, as always, thanks to Debbie Block for listening and reading.

Chapter One

"That new teacher Mrs. Tibbets is a hundred years old, you'll see!" Frankie announces.

"*Two* hundred years old!" another boy says.

Ben Moroney ignores them as he heads down the hall. Jenny Ferreira is walking beside him. The other kids in his fifth-grade class are stretched out in a loose line up and down the hallway, headed to science class.

"Mrs. Tibbets isn't that old," Jenny tells Ben. "And she's not a new teacher. She's just been out for a while. My brother had her in fifth grade a couple of years ago."

Ben nods. He likes Jenny. She's one of the few kids who talk to him—maybe just because he sits behind her in class. He's been at Edenboro Elementary School for two months but he still feels new. Now they've got a new science teacher, too. She's new to Ben, at least. Everybody else in the class seems to know her.

"She's a *million* years old!" Frankie shouts so everyone in the hall can hear. He bends over and hobbles down the hall like an old woman, and Tommy Miller and Dennis Dimeo laugh. Frankie thinks he's a lot funnier than he is, but there are always kids who'll laugh at him. Even when he's being mean.

It's strange to get a new science teacher at the end of March. Ben wonders where Mrs. Tibbets has been and—more importantly—why she came back.

When Ben walks into the classroom, he doesn't see the science teacher.

But he does see the mice.

They're in a new cage on a table against the back wall, next to stacks of textbooks and papers. He figures there are half a dozen mice in it.

Ben knows something about mice, but not as pets. He knows about mice as food for diamondback rattlesnakes. He's seen rattlesnakes eat mice lots of times.

There are no diamondback rattlesnakes in Edenboro, Massachusetts. Ben's pretty sure of that. The rattlesnakes he used to watch were at the Desert Museum in Tucson, Arizona, where he lived until February. Along with whipsnakes and sidewinders. And horned toads. And chuckwalla lizards. All he's seen since they moved to Massachusetts are some squirrels and chipmunks in his backyard and some birds at the window feeder.

Ben walks toward the cage to get a closer look at the mice. Ryan Brisson starts pounding on a desk not far from the table. "Ben! Ben!" he yells. "Sit here!" With a new teacher, there aren't any rules yet, and everyone is thinking they can sit anywhere they want. Frankie, Tommy, and Dennis have claimed desks all together on the other side of the room.

Ryan's a skinny little kid who wears glasses. One of the lenses is covered over with a patch, and the other lens magnifies his good eye. He's always peering at people out of that one big eye. He's the most hyper kid that Ben has ever met. It's like his mother gives him a pound of sugar right before he leaves for school every day. He drives Ben crazy. He drives the other kids crazy. He even drives the teachers crazy.

Ben wishes he had a real friend. Not like Jenny, who only talks to him because she sits in front of him. Or Ryan, who is officially wacko. He'd like to find someone like Toby, his best friend back in Tucson.

"Sit here!" Ryan says again, pounding on the desk like a bass drum. "It's the only empty seat!" The kid is a human noise machine. He'd be noisy even if he were sitting still. Which he never is.

Ben glances around the classroom. The new teacher, Mrs. Tibbets, hasn't arrived yet. Teachers are usually pretty good about not leaving a classroom unattended, but sometimes it happens. He looks at the mice again, then thinks about Mr. Tompkins, the director of the children's programs at the

Desert Museum. Ben loved that museum. He'd taken every summer class they offered for his age group, and he'd talked his parents into taking him there almost every Saturday during the school year.

Mr. Tompkins had promised Ben that when he was a little older he could help out with one of the summer programs. But then in December, Ben's dad was offered a new job, and two months later his family packed up and left Tucson. Now he's stuck here looking at mice in Massachusetts.

He doesn't even have his souvenirs from the museum. The box that held his favorite things from his bedroom got lost in the move, and the moving company can't find it.

Ryan is still pounding the desk, calling for Ben, but it's like the kid has forgotten what he really wants and now just enjoys the sound of his own pounding and chanting.

"Here, here, here!" he's saying.

"Ryan Brisson!" Frankie Mirley shouts out in a creaky voice. "Ryan Brisson, could you kindly shut your trap for once in your life?" He's still imitating an old woman. Dennis and Tommy and a couple of other boys who always laugh at Frankie's jokes let out loud guffaws.

Mrs. Tibbets still hasn't arrived, and the kids are all standing up talking and making noise. The longer there's not a teacher in the room, the wilder it gets. Even the mice in the cage are agitated now, running around like the students in the room. Ben knows how to handle mice. He undoes the latch, reaches in and scoops one up in his hand, then latches the door shut. He lets the mouse run from one hand to another, putting each hand in front of the one that's holding it.

"Hey, wow! What're you doing?" Ryan jumps out of his seat and skips over to where Ben is holding the mouse. "Are you supposed to do that?"

"No way," another kid says. "Old Mrs. Tibbets'll kill you. They're probably for a science experiment or something."

Other kids gather around. Ben is holding the mouse close to his face, looking at its twitching nose and bright eyes. He thinks about how the workers at the museum fed the mice to snakes. At first he was upset, but Mr. Tompkins had explained that it was all part of the cycle of life. "It's sad," he'd said, "but all species depend on other forms of life to live. That's why there are so many mice—to make sure the species survives. Of course, we're at the top of the food chain. There are a lot of us, but that's because there's no one to eat us."

"You should put it back," Jenny says to Ben, "before Mrs. Tibbets gets here." She's twisting her fingers in her hair, like she's the one who's going to get in trouble.

"It's okay," Ben says. "I just want to see it for a minute."

Ryan reaches for the mouse, trying to get it out of Ben's hands. "Let me hold him!" he says. "I'll be careful."

"No, Ryan," Ben says, twisting around to shield the mouse. Ryan manages to grab Ben's wrist with one hand.

"Wait!" Ben yells. But Ryan clamps down on the little animal with his other hand. Afraid the mouse will be crushed, Ben lets go.

Ryan lifts it up in the air like it's a trophy or something. "I've got it!" he shrieks. "It's squirmy!"

"Well, duh," Frankie sneers.

"Well, duh," three other boys echo.

Ryan tries to hold on to the mouse, but it crawls out of his hands and runs down his arm. "Aaaaaah!" he yells, and the whole class starts screaming.

The mouse leaps off Ryan's arm, lands on the floor, and skitters under the desks, looking for a safe place to hide. But there's no safe place—not with a bunch of fifth graders after it.

"Get it! Get it!" Frankie shouts in his old woman's voice. "Killer mouse on the loose!" Three or four kids squeal and run to the opposite side of the room, like it really is a killer mouse and might hurt them.

"It climbed down my arm! Get it! Get it!" Ryan is dancing around the circle of kids who are on their hands and knees looking for the mouse. Three or four of them corner it in the front of the room. "I'll get it!" Ben says, pushing his way through the crowd. He's about to scoop it up when another voice yells out and everybody freezes where they are.

"WHAT IS GOING ON IN HERE?"

Ben turns to see a woman standing in the door of the classroom.

There's a moment when nobody says anything, and then everybody runs to their seats, trying not to laugh, even though they know they're in trouble—it's funny and scary at the same time. Now is Ben's chance to catch the mouse, so he kneels down and scoops it up, then turns to face the teacher.

Mrs. Tibbets is an older woman, but nowhere near a hundred years old. She stands straight and tall, not bent over at all. Ben is never good at guessing how old grown-ups are, but he figures she's about as old as his Grandmother Moroney. Her long, graying hair is pulled back behind her ears in a braid that reaches partway down her back. She's wearing a bulky wool sweater and a long skirt, but the most interesting thing about her is her feet. She's wearing a pair of old leather hiking boots. Ben has never seen a teacher in hiking boots.

Before anybody can say anything else, Frankie stands and points at Ben. "He let the mouse out!" Frankie sounds happy. A lot of people like to see other people get in trouble, but Frankie *loves* it. "He let the mouse out. I told him not to!"

Mrs. Tibbets looks at Ben with her eyes squinted a little.

Ben holds the mouse up in his hands. He can feel his own heart beating. "It's okay. I caught it," he says.

"Put it back in the cage, please," she says. "Everyone in their seats."

The entire classroom watches as Ben walks across the room. He opens the cage door and slips the mouse back in. The rescued animal scurries around the cage, jumps over a couple of other mice until it reaches a corner, and huddles there like nothing unusual has happened.

Mrs. Tibbets tells Ben to find a seat and walks over to the small teacher's desk in front of her class.

"Here, Ben!" shouts Ryan, pounding on the desk next to his. "Sit here!"

There's nowhere else to sit, so Ben slides into the vacant desk. Ryan gives him a lopsided smile. Ben looks away. He feels like he's balancing on a tightrope, trying to be nice to Ryan, but not too nice. Ben doesn't want to be mean, but the kid is too hyper to be a good friend. And Ben knows that being nice to Frankie's favorite victim will make him a target, too. It's enough to make his head hurt.

Mrs. Tibbets writes her name on the board and stands at the front of the class for a moment, waiting. It gets very quiet. Even Ryan seems to be holding still, which is a minor miracle.

"My name is Mrs. Tibbets, and I'll be teaching you science for the rest of the year. Most of you probably know I've been a teacher here at Edenboro for many years. I took a little time off, and now I'm back."

The teacher walks back to the front of her desk, taking her time. Ben sneaks another glance at her hiking boots.

"I expect you to sit in your seats the moment you come to class, whether I'm here or not." She pauses and looks around. "And please do not touch anything in the room unless you ask my permission. Especially animals in cages. Animals are living things and need to be treated carefully. They're not toys."

Frankie turns and looks at Ben and wags his finger. Mrs. Tibbets walks over and puts a hand on his shoulder.

"Augh!" Frankie squawks, like he's being strangled. Dennis laughs. Mrs. Tibbets glares at Frankie, then returns to the board at the front of the class. She writes down a bunch of words and asks the kids to copy them into their notebooks so they can look them up for homework. Ben wonders why she just doesn't hand out a sheet with the words on them. While the kids are writing down the words, Mrs. Tibbets patrols the aisles. When Mrs. Tibbets passes by Ben's desk, he notices that her hiking boots are a little muddy. He wonders if she walked to school or something, and he looks back over at the mice again.

Mrs. Tibbets walks down the row of desks, then turns up the next aisle. When she gets to Ben's desk again, she leans over his paper.

"I finished," Ben says. She reaches out with her wrinkled hand and jabs a short, cracked fingernail at a word on his paper. *Mrs. Kutcher has fingernail polish on her fingernails,* Ben thinks. *Not Mrs. Tibbets.* Ben looks at the word under her finger. He sees that he has accidentally left the *t* out of *nocturnal.* He already knows what the word means—something that comes out at night. He fixes the spelling.

The teacher leans over the desk a little farther and asks in a soft voice, "What is your name?"

"Ben," he says. "Ben Moroney." Mrs. Tibbets's sweater doesn't smell like school. It smells like the outdoors. Like wood smoke and fresh air.

"Good," she says, looking right at him. The lines around her eyes and mouth turn down a little, making her look sad. "Ben, please don't touch those mice again. Do you understand me?"

Ben feels his face get hot. He nods, but he wants to defend himself, too. "I've taken care of mice before," he mutters. "I know about them."

"They're not pets," she says.

"I know how to hold them," Ben says, but Mrs. Tibbets has already straightened up and is starting to walk away.

"If they're not pets, what are they for?" Ben asks a little louder, and a couple of kids turn around and look back at him.

Mrs. Tibbets looks back at him, too, her eyebrows raised. Ben can feel that's he's pushing it a little, but he wants to know.

"Are they for bait, or food, or maybe for an experiment? I know someone who feeds mice to snakes. Is it something like that?" he asks. Now everybody is watching Mrs. Tibbets to see how she's going to react.

Ben waits for her to get mad. But she doesn't. Her lips

scrunch up, almost like she's trying not to smile. "Go over the words one more time, Ben," she says. "I brought the mice in to show the second graders. And we're not talking about snakes today. Maybe some other day."

Mrs. Tibbets goes back to the front of the room and begins to talk about the differences between warm-blooded and cold-blooded animals. Ben is only half listening—he already knows all that. But he hears a word that makes his heart skip a beat in his chest.

"*Snakes.*"

He looks back at the mice again and then up at Mrs. Tibbets, with her gray hair and cracked fingernails and baggy sweater.

And hiking boots.

Chapter Two

Geography is the last class of the day. Ben stares out of the classroom window at the rain beating against the glass. He can hear it on the roof, too, and see it making the puddles on the playground dance. It's rained or snowed or sleeted just about every day since he moved to Massachusetts.

Mrs. Kutcher holds up a sheet of paper. "This is the most important project of the year," she says. "We've been studying different ecosystems and biomes all year, and now you get to choose your favorite one. You'll need to use your reading and writing and research skills and everything you've learned about different ecosystems. You'll have two months to do it, but you should start working on it now. A project this big can't be done at the last minute."

Mrs. Kutcher gives the first person in each row a stack of

information pages to pass back. Ben stares at Jenny's long, black hair while he waits. It's always straight and neat, like she brushes it a thousand times every morning. Jenny takes a sheet, then turns to hand the stack to Ben with a smile. She has a gap between her two front teeth that makes her smiles relaxed and friendly, which seems different from her neat, combed hair.

Jenny turns back and picks up the book she was reading. She's a book sponge. Some kids read one book every two weeks. She reads one every other day. In fact, she reads so much that she gets in trouble for it, which seems pretty funny to Ben. Teachers are always telling you how important reading is, and then when you actually read a lot, you get in trouble for it. But Jenny's head is always buried in a book, and it's usually a book that doesn't have anything to do with what they're studying. Mrs. Kutcher almost always has a book on her desk that she's taken away from Jenny during health or geography or even reading.

Jenny is smart in a very weird way—not in the way of always doing exactly the right thing in school. She's smart in seeing the world in a way others don't, like she has her head tilted to one side a little and looks at the world from a different angle.

Jenny turns back to Ben again, still wearing her gap-toothed grin. "What did Mrs. Tibbets say to you?" she whispers.

Ben shrugs.

"Did you get in trouble?"

Ben shakes his head. "I don't think so. It seemed like she was mad, but then she didn't do anything. She told me not to touch the mice."

"I wonder what she uses them for. My brother—"

"Excuse me, Jenny," Mrs. Kutcher interrupts their conversation. "Could you please turn around and pay attention? I'm not just talking to hear my own voice."

Jenny gives Ben another quick smile and turns around. Ben feels his face turn red. He looks at the assignment sheet.

Geography Project: Exploring World Ecosystems

Your major report for the spring will be on an ecosystem anywhere in the world. In the report you should explain the following:

- *what and where the ecosystem is*
- *what the climate is like*
- *which plants and animals are part of it*
- *how it fits in with the other ecosystems of the world.*

Please also discuss what makes the ecosystem a unique place and what threatens it. The report should be three to five pages in length. Please include artwork, charts, or models that will help us understand the special nature of your habitat.

You may choose your own topic or ask me for help in selecting one.

The project is due Friday, June 5.

Ben knows right away what topic he wants to do. Other kids are looking at their papers, and some are already waving their hands in the air.

"Mrs. Kutcher, can I do the rain forest in Costa Rica?" Jenny asks.

The teacher nods. "That's what *I* wanted to do," someone whines without waiting to be called on. Three or four other kids join in, like the rain forest is the only interesting place in the world.

Frankie Mirley shouts out, "I want the beach! Where I can see bikinis!"

His buddies break out laughing. Mrs. Kutcher shoots Frankie a look, but he doesn't seem to care; he's scored points with his friends.

Ben isn't interested in the rain forest or the beach. He shoots his hand up in the air, and Mrs. Kutcher calls on him.

"Can I do the desert?" he asks. "The Sonoran Desert in Arizona?"

"Sure," says Mrs. Kutcher. "You must know a lot about that already."

Ben nods.

"Whoever heard of a snoring desert?" Frankie shouts, and the same crew of boys snickers.

"So-no-ran." Ben pronounces the word slowly. "It's the name of the desert around where I lived in Tucson."

"So-no-ran, sno-ring," Frankie sneers. "Whatever. It's all he ever talks about. Who cares about Toooo-sahn anyway?"

Ben pretends he doesn't hear. Jenny looks back at Ben and rolls her eyes. He shrugs.

He wonders if it's true. Is it all he talks about? *Maybe so*, he thinks. *And it's no wonder. Tucson sure was better than here. Especially with kids like Frankie around.* Finally he sneaks a glance at Frankie, who's smirking at his friends. Tommy Miller reaches across the aisle and gives him a high five.

Jenny mouths these words to Ben: "He's an idiot."

Mrs. Kutcher raises her voice, trying to get the class back on track. "That's enough for now. I'll have a little conference with each of you to find out what you'd like to do. I have a list of ecosystems, and I'm sure each of you can find an interesting one that no one else is doing." She looks at the clock and says, "Okay, class, pack your things. It's nearly time to go."

"All the way to the 'snoring desert,'" Frankie taunts.

You can't win with Frankie and Ben knows it. He keeps his mouth shut and concentrates on stuffing his notebooks and books in his backpack.

By the time Ben gets on the bus, most of the seats are taken. All of the fifth graders are in the back of the bus where they always sit. Ryan's back there, too, and calls to him, but Ben chooses a seat halfway back, with a third grader he doesn't know.

Ben's sister Agatha is on the bus, too. She's sitting in the front with Rory, Ryan's sister—they're both in second grade. Agatha and Rory are laughing and talking with the kids in the seat behind them as the bus pulls out of the school circle, and Ben wonders why it's so easy for his sister to make friends. It's like she's lived in Edenboro forever. Maybe it's because she talks so much. Ben looks out the window. He doesn't see that much point in talking unless it's about something important.

At about the third stop on the route, Ryan lurches down the aisle. When he gets to Ben's seat, he peers down at him with his good eye. "See ya tomorrow, Ben!"

Ben nods, then quickly looks out the window again.

Then Ben hears Frankie's voice. "Arrrr, Captain Kidd! Captain Kidd! Good-bye, Captain Kidd!"

Ben can't help looking back. Frankie's got a hand over one eye like it's a patch. A couple of other boys are laughing. Ben turns in time to see Ryan getting off the bus—his head is down and his ears are bright red. Frankie and his buddies are already ragging on one of the fourth graders.

When the bus comes to a stop at the end of Ben's street, he steps out the door into the drizzling rain. Agatha is waiting for him at the bottom of the stairs.

"Come on, Ben. Let's run!"

"I'm not running. You can if you want."

"But Mom said we have to walk together," Agatha says in that whiny little-sister voice she was born with.

"Then we can walk," Ben answers.

"But we'll get wet!"

"Agatha, go ahead and run if you want. I'm walking."

"Poophead," his sister says. She whirls around and takes off down the street. Ben holds his backpack on top of his head to keep the rain off and plods toward his house. The entire sky is gray and some of the puddles on the street are deep. His feet get wet, even though he's watching where he's stepping. The grass in the yards is beginning to turn green again, but there are no leaves on the trees yet. He peers up from under his backpack. The tree branches hang over the street—there are tons more trees here than in Arizona. He tries to imagine all the branches filled with leaves.

Ben cuts across a yard to avoid a big puddle on the sidewalk. The ground is like a soaked sponge—the water wells up around his shoes. The smell of the wet earth fills the heavy air. He's never seen this much water lying around before. The desert has gentle rains in the winter and hard, huge thunderstorms in the summer, but the rain soaks into the dry earth or runs off in a matter of hours. It never stays around for long.

Ben used to love the big thunderstorms. He could always smell them coming. The wind whipped up in front of them, as the storms rolled across the desert floor and the clouds rose higher and higher in the sky. *Out there everything races and crashes and breathes like it's a living thing,* he thinks. *Here in Massachusetts the rain just goes on and on. Nothing very exciting about that.*

Thinking about the thunderstorms reminds Ben of the things from his bedroom that got lost in the move. He'd collected most of them himself, but some of the best stuff came from the Desert Museum. Mr. Thompson had given him a rabbit skull and a fossil of a trilobite, a sea creature from millions of years ago. But his favorite thing was the shed skin from a king snake. Ben had watched the snake in the display case at the museum for over an hour while it wriggled out of its old skin and left it behind. Its head and body emerged with new skin that was bright and shiny and vibrant. It was one of the most amazing things Ben had ever seen. Mr. Thompson gave him the dried old crinkly skin that stretched out even longer than the three-foot snake itself.

But it wasn't just the displays and creatures in the museum that made it so great. Even better were all the things he learned there about the desert. And the more he knew, the more he wanted to know. Every time he went to the museum he peppered Mr. Thompson and the other guides with a thousand questions.

"Ben," his mother had said, "you'll drive them crazy!"

But Mr. Thompson and the others seemed happy to share what they knew. "That's what we're here for!" the old man had said. The guides taught Ben to be watchful and patient when he was outside. "Nature shows itself when you give it time.

There are a lot of critters out there," Mr. Thompson had said, "and you'll see them if you know how to be still and wait."

Ben had learned to be patient. In Arizona, he'd grab a snack after school and then walk down to the river wash at the end of his street. There were new houses going up, but behind them there was just open space, the desert stretching out and up into the foothills of the mountains west of Tucson. After the area's big thunderstorms, the river ran through the wash, creating a lush place for trees and plants that wouldn't last a week in the dry ground a hundred yards away.

Ben had a favorite waiting place in the river wash: a big rock in the shade of a cottonwood tree. He would sit there not moving at all, and after a while he'd always see something. Mice were regulars, and ground squirrels and lizards. Sometimes he saw javelinas—small wild pigs—snorting and scurrying from one bush to another. And on a few lucky occasions, he saw snakes. The more he watched and waited, the more animals he saw and learned to identify.

One Saturday when he was home, he heard his mother give a little yelp as she walked into the laundry room. Ben ran to see what was wrong.

"It's a frog!" she said, pointing in the corner.

Ben looked closely. "No, Mom. It's a toad!" he said. "It's a Colorado River toad!"

"I don't care what it is," his mother said. "I don't want it anywhere near my washing machine."

The large squat toad sat in the corner, looking perfectly happy to be there. "He won't hurt anything," Ben said. "He'll eat the spiders."

Ben talked his parents into leaving the toad there for a several days. He was happy, and so was the toad, but his mom wasn't. Ben finally carefully scooped it into a box, took it back down to the river wash, and let it go.

"Ben's Toad Removal!" his father had quipped.

In Arizona Ben spent as much time outside as he could. Most of the kids from school were busy doing other things, either playing sports or staying inside with their computers and TVs. But Ben didn't really like team sports, although he was big for his age and people always wanted him on their teams. And he couldn't stand spending too much time inside. It made him feel like he was wasting the day, wasting the sun. He liked being outside by himself, or with someone who liked the outdoors as much as he did. Toby was the only other kid he knew who was happy spending the day exploring the nearby desert.

Ben and Toby had started a collection of things they'd found. They got a terrarium and put things in it and named it Desert World. They filled the bottom with sand and some rocks, then planted a few small cactuses and turned it into a sort of ant farm. An ant and stinkbug farm, actually. Ben loved catching stinkbugs, funny little critters that lifted their back ends high in the air when they thought they were being attacked. But the main inhabitant of Desert World was Lenny, a western banded gecko. Toby and Ben had spent hours watching the small, quick lizard as it scurried around its little home, dining on the stinkbugs and grasshoppers they fed it.

But Ben had to leave all that behind in Tucson. Now Toby was caring for Lenny and everything else in Desert World.

Maybe, Ben thinks, *the moving people have found the box and I'll get my collection of rocks and bugs back, and my books and posters.*

Chapter Three

By the time Ben reaches his driveway, his sneakers are soaked. He splashes in every puddle on the way up the driveway and comes in the side door into the kitchen. Agatha's already sitting at the kitchen table, having a snack. She's got crackers lined up carefully on one side of her place mat and slices of cheese on the other, and she's putting them together one at a time, singing a song she made up:

"Cracker, cracker, cracker.
Cheese, cheese, cheese.
Put them both together.
Remember not to sneeze."

"Dumb song," Ben says.

"I know," she says. It doesn't bother her at all.

She stops her cracker-and-cheese game and holds up a

note. “This says that Mom will be home in an hour,” Agatha announces. “She left us cheese and crackers.”

“Let me see,” Ben says, reaching for the note. He reads it, hoping it will say something about his missing box. No such luck. Nothing but crackers and cheese, and do the chores. Ben tosses his backpack on a kitchen chair and walks through the house, looking to see if the box has arrived. He runs up the stairs to his bedroom. No box there either. The room feels empty and lonely. The walls are bare except for a Boston Red Sox poster his father put up. Ben has always been an Arizona Diamondbacks fan, but his dad has promised to take him to see the Red Sox.

“Darn!” Ben says loudly, wishing somebody was there to hear. “It didn’t come.” Now he’s in a bad mood. He goes back downstairs and heads to the kitchen for his snack.

Agatha has finished her snack. She’s brushing the cracker crumbs into a pile in the middle of her place mat. “Wanna play a game?” she asks.

“No,” Ben says. He doesn’t feel like any kind of game. “Where’s the rest of the crackers and cheese?”

“I ate them. I thought you didn’t want any because you went upstairs.”

Ben groans and opens a cabinet door. He pulls out a box of cereal and pours some out in his hand, then wolfs it down dry.

“Wanna watch TV?”

"We're not supposed to on school days," Ben says. "You know that."

"Wanna draw pictures?"

"No."

"Wanna say 'no' all the time?"

Agatha is just trying to be annoying. She has radar that tells her exactly how to annoy her older brother. "What I want is for you to be quiet for once," he says.

"I can't. It's impossible. I have to breathe and breathing makes sound. So I can't be quiet."

"Maybe you could stop breathing."

"Maybe you're a grouch," Agatha says.

"Because you're a pest!" Ben shouts. He looks out the kitchen window. If it were Tucson, he'd go outside. But he can't leave Agatha alone, and it's raining anyway. He's trapped. "HELP!" he bellows. "I'M TRAPPED IN MASSACHUSETTS IN A HOUSE WITH A DUMB SISTER!"

"I'M TRAPPED WITH A DUMBER BROTHER!" Agatha yells back. She's having a great time.

"I may have to hang you by your feet," Ben mutters.

"You're not allowed to!" Agatha says. "Dad said so."

Ben turns on the TV. His parents have strict rules about TV during the school week, but he's so annoyed he doesn't care. Agatha hears it and comes in the room.

"Hey," she says, "you said not to watch TV and now you're doing it."

"It's so I don't murder you."

"You can't murder me either," Agatha says. "It's against the law." She sits on the floor and stares at the screen. Before Ben knows it they're both lost in the program, and then his mother is standing in the doorway of the family room.

"Why is the television on?" she asks.

"Ben turned it on," says Agatha.

"What's going on here, Ben?" his mother asks. "You know the rules."

"I know," he says, "but Agatha was driving me crazy, and we can't go outside because it's raining like always, and I couldn't find my box of stuff. Did it come?"

"No," she says.

"Did you call the moving company again?"

"I forgot," his mother says.

"Mom!" Ben can hear the whine in his voice, but he can't help it.

"I'm sorry, Ben. I'll call them in a minute. Did you have a snack yet?"

"Someone did," Ben says, glaring at Agatha. His mother goes up to the TV set to turn it off, but before she gets there, Ben flicks it off with the remote.

"Do you have much homework?" she asks.

"Just some dumb math problems," he says.

"Why don't you do it now?"

"I don't feel like it." He gets up from the couch and starts to walk out of the room.

"Oh, Ben," his mother exclaims. "Your shoes are all muddy!"

"That's because I live in a rain forest," Ben says.

"He's a big grouch," Agatha says. "Ever since we moved here he's a big, grumpy grouch."

Ben is out of the room now, but he hears what his sister is saying. "I wonder why," he yells back. "Maybe because I hate this place?"

"Ben!" His mother is mad now, and Ben knows it. It takes a lot to make her mad, and now he's on the verge of some serious trouble. But he doesn't stop. He has to get out of the house.

He doesn't care if it's still raining.

He doesn't care if his feet are wet and muddy.

He doesn't care about anything but getting away for a while.

He pulls on his hooded jacket and goes out the kitchen door. He figures he'll have to pay for yelling and walking out when he gets back. But he doesn't care.

The rain splatters on the hood of his jacket as he circles around to the back of the house and stands there looking across the yard. It stretches twenty-five yards to a line of tall trees. Beyond that the land slopes gently downward to some woods. Ben's been back there once or twice, but he's never gotten very far because the ground is so soggy. Now he doesn't care if it's soggy. He just wants to go somewhere. Anywhere.

He slogs across the lawn and passes underneath the trees. He squeezes through the shrubs that mark the back edge of the yard and peers into the woods. It's getting darker, but he can see what looks like a faint path.

A path he's never noticed before.

His heart beating fast, he starts down the path. The rain trickles off his hood onto his nose and seeps through the shoulders of his jacket. He doesn't care. So what if he gets soaked?

He walks slowly, willing himself to calm down and stay quiet. After a few yards his heartbeat returns to a normal pace and his mind stops racing quite so much. Then he stops. Did he hear something? He stands still and listens. It wasn't the rain hitting the branches overhead. Or the sound of his feet scuffing the wet ground. Or even his breathing.

The faint noise begins again. It sounds like something calling. Something living. A little shudder runs down Ben's spine, but he follows the path, moving farther away from the house. He has to fight his way through the underbrush, and twice he has to double back to find a place where his sneakers don't sink down into the muddy ground. Guided by the sounds, he pushes through to an open space that's even wetter. Thin trees stand lone and bare in several shallow pools, where the raindrops are making circles upon circles on the surface. Here and there he sees green clumps of moss, but otherwise everything is brown and gray.

Ben stands still. It's now completely silent again. He likes being out here by himself. It's not the desert, but he's alone and outside. He doesn't mind the rain. His feet are cold and wet, but they'll get dry again. Ben listens. He shivers a little, wondering how long he can stay outside and what he'll say when he gets back to the house.

It's getting darker.

Then he hears it. One silvery whistle. A chirp. A peep.

Ben listens harder. It's not a bird. It sounds again. And then, very close to him, another one sounds. He turns to look but can't see anything.

The noise seems to be coming from a clump of dead grass sticking out of the marsh. It's a clear, bell-like chirp, rising in pitch. It seems out of place in this dull, gray landscape.

Then something moves at his feet.

Ben almost jumps out of his skin. But when he looks down he can't see anything. A tingle goes up the back of his neck. Maybe it's a snake.

Then it moves again, and Ben makes out a camouflaged shape among the brown and dirty green of the earth and plants. He leans over.

It's a frog.

He picks it up.

Ben holds the creature in his hand until it calms down.

He cups it with one hand and uses the fingers of his other to hold it carefully right in front of the back legs, like they showed him at the Desert Museum. It squirms in his hand, but Ben doesn't let go.

He looks at it closely. He knows it's a frog and not a toad. Its skin is smooth and its legs are long. He has no idea what kind of frog it is—he's never seen one like it before. It's got ridges on its back and a black mask around its eyes, like a bandit.

The rain continues to fall. His sneakers feel heavy and squishy on his feet. Ben strokes the frog's back, wondering if this was the thing that made the silvery chirp he had just heard. He holds the frog up to his face and looks at it closely. It just sits there. It doesn't seem to care if Ben holds him or not. Ben knows the frog is sluggish because it's cold-blooded—like snakes or lizards, it can't move very fast when it's really cold. The frog flattens itself in his hand.

"Be-en! Ben-benny-ben-ben!"

Ben hears his father's voice calling through the growing darkness. He's singing the name like it's part of a song, and Ben can't help but smile. His father is a great joker, and it sounds like he's in a good mood. The beam from a flashlight bobs up and down in the distance, coming toward him. In the dark, it almost looks like a ghost. Ben shivers again. It's time to go back.

Just as he's getting ready to plop the frog back in the puddle, Ben thinks of Mrs. Tibbets, with her long gray hair and hiking boots. He wonders what she would think of what he just found. He cradles the creature in both hands a moment longer, then slips it into his jacket pocket.

"Come on, Mr. Frog," he says. "Pack your bags, it's time to move." Then he calls out, "Coming!" and plunges through the bushes and back onto the path. He finds his dad walking toward him, still wearing his office suit and his good raincoat. It seems funny to see him in the middle of a swamp in dress clothes.

"Hey, you goofball," his father says. "Your mother sent me out here to find you. Have you noticed it's raining?" He puts his arm around Ben's shoulder and turns toward the house.

"I was listening," says Ben.

"To what? The rain?"

Ben guesses his father isn't going to talk to him about yelling at his mom, which is good.

"No. I was listening to something making a weird sound. Like this high-pitched peeping."

"Probably a killer snake," his father says.

"Dad, there are no killer snakes here."

"Yes, there are," his father says in a serious tone that shows he's kidding. "I happen to know they lie out here in this swamp behind our house and they're eight feet long and they make peeping sounds right before they swallow boys who are dumb enough to stand out in the rain."

"C'mon, Dad," Ben says. "There was really something out there. You can hear it if you stop."

Ben stops walking and so does his father. The peeps sound faintly in the wet air.

"There! Hear them?"

"Definitely killer snakes," his father says. "Huge ones."

Ben laughs. "Snakes don't make noises like that!"

"Suit yourself. But don't blame me if one swallows you up. Your mother probably won't mind. One less kid to worry about."

Ben doesn't respond. They start walking again.

"So, what's up with school?" his father asks.

"Oh, it's okay," Ben says. He puts his hand on the outside of his coat pocket and feels the shape of the frog inside.

"Just okay, huh?"

Ben doesn't want to talk about school. "Dad, what if you don't like your job here?"

"Well, the good news is that I do like it."

"But what if you didn't? Or it didn't work out just right? Would we move back home to Tucson?"

"No."

"How come?"

"Because I hate packing."

"Really, how come?"

"Ben, pal. This is our home now. We're staying here." His father pulls Ben close as they come in the backyard, but Ben slips out of the hug. He doesn't want to be close.

Not if they have to stay here.

While everyone else is getting ready for dinner, Ben goes out in the garage and hunts around until he finds a small plastic bucket. He takes the frog out of his pocket and puts it in the bucket, then covers it with a small window screen he finds leaning against the garage wall.

"I don't have a good place for you, fella," he says, squatting down for a closer look. The frog sits in the bottom of the bucket, not moving. Ben thinks about taking the bucket in the house, but changes his mind. He doesn't want to explain it to Mom or have Agatha bugging him about it. Besides, he likes the idea of having something that's just his and no one else's. He decides to leave it in the garage. He'll find a better place for it tomorrow.

"At least it's warmer here than outside," he says to the frog, which doesn't seem to care where it is. Ben turns off the garage lights and goes inside.

After dinner Ben goes into his bedroom to do his homework. He's barely sat down when the phone rings.

"I'll get it," Ben yells, almost knocking his chair over in his hurry to get to the phone. He grabs the receiver away just as Agatha picks it up.

"Hey, no fair!" she whines, but Ben's already got the phone to his ear.

He covers the mouthpiece. "Life's not fair!" he says. She sticks out her tongue, and Ben speaks into the phone. "Hello?"

"Hey, Snakeman," says a voice on the other end.

Ben laughs. "Toby!"

"Wrong, Snakeman. This is Lizardman." Tony is talking in a creepy, croaky voice that cracks Ben up. It makes him more homesick than ever.

"Hi, Toby. How's Lenny?" Ben asks.

"He's fine. Eating stinkbugs and sleeping. How's everything in Massachusetts?"

"It stinks worse than the bugs. It's cold and wet. And the kids here are idiots."

"Wow. That's too bad."

"Yeah," Ben agrees. "But maybe we won't stay here for too long. Maybe we'll move back!"

"That'd be great. I could sure use your help. Larry Dunstan has been bugging the heck out of me."

"Ooooh, not him!" Ben snorts.

"Yeah. What a turkey."

They both laugh. They talk and talk until Ben's mother taps him on the shoulder.

"That's enough," she says. "You've got homework."

"Mom!" he pleads.

"It's enough for now. You can call back in a couple of days."

"I gotta go, Lizardman," Ben says. "Thanks for calling. I'll e-mail you. And I'll call next week. Or you can call me."

"Okay, pal. Stay in touch. Don't let those Massachusetts kids bug you."

Ben hangs up the phone. He wonders how talking to Toby can make him happy and sad at the same time. He goes to the computer in the family room and writes an e-mail to Toby.

lizardman,

please rescue me from the monsters in massachusetts.

only you can save me.

desert creatures unite!

snakeman :~~~~~~~~~~~~~

Chapter Four

The next day after school Ben checks on the frog in the bucket. It's still just sitting there, and it doesn't seem very happy. It doesn't seem very much of anything. He feels bad. He knows he should let it go, but he doesn't want to yet. He takes a plastic grocery bag and a garden trowel into the backyard, where he digs up some dirt, grass, and wet leaves. Next he wanders out under the big trees and finds some worms under an old log. He plops them into the bag. Then he takes his bag back to the garage and puts the things he's gathered into the bucket with the frog.

It's not much of a home, he thinks, *but it'll have to do for now.*

The next morning, a few minutes before time to leave for the bus stop, Ben goes out into the garage to check on the frog. It doesn't seem to have moved since the night before. He feels bad leaving it there all day, so he picks it up and slips it in his jacket again. It'll be fun having a secret frog in his pocket.

By the time he gets to school, he wonders what he was thinking. Was he nuts? What do you do with a frog in school? Ben doesn't want to be there—why would a frog want to be there, either? He's afraid to leave the jacket hanging on the peg in the coatroom, so he keeps it on. Mrs. Kutcher asks him to take it off, but Ben tells her he's cold. All through the morning he keeps checking his pocket. The frog just sits there, barely moving. Once when Ben puts his hand in his pocket, the frog squirms a little like it's trying to get away.

"It's okay, buddy," he whispers. "At least it's warm in there."

Today Mrs. Kutcher leads the kids down to science class. Mrs. Tibbets isn't in the classroom again, but there's a note on the door saying she's working with the first graders on the other side of the school. Mrs. Kutcher looks at the note and says, "All right, class, you're all fifth graders and know how to behave yourselves. Have a seat until Mrs. Tibbets is back."

Everyone takes their seats. Mrs. Kutcher watches them for a moment, then turns and walks down the hall.

The class is alone again. Everyone sits at their desks quietly for about thirty seconds. Then they all start talking.

Ben checks his pocket again.

Ryan notices. "What're you doing?"

It's too good a secret to keep. Ben wants to share it with someone, even if it's only Ryan. He pulls out the frog. As soon as he does, he realizes it's a mistake. Nothing stays a secret with Ryan for long. The kid leaps from his desk and hops over to Ben's on one foot.

"Cool! A frog! Where'd you get it?"

"Shhhhh." Ben tries to calm Ryan down. "I found it behind my house."

"What're you going to do with it?"

"I don't know. Just keep it, I guess."

"Why don't you scare somebody with it?" Ryan asks. "Or put it down someone's back? Here, let me hold it." Ryan reaches for it, just like he did the mouse.

"I've got to put it back," Ben says, but Ryan already has his fingers on the frog. "Ryan, no!"

Ryan's not listening. He can't listen. It's exactly like what happened the other day. What is wrong with this kid?

Other kids gather around to see what's going on. Ben pulls the frog away from Ryan, but it wriggles out of his hands. It falls to the floor and sits there.

Frankie pounces. "Got it!" he yells. He holds it up and starts to run around the room with it. He shoves it in Janice Decker's face. "Here! Kiss it! Give the toadie a little kiss!"

"Stop it!" she squeals.

"C'mon, Frankie, give it back," Ben pleads. "It's not yours. And it doesn't like that!"

"Poor toadie. Doesn't like kissing girls!" Frankie turns so Ben can't reach the frog and laughs hysterically.

"WHAT'S GOING ON NOW?" Mrs. Tibbets's voice rings out. Everybody stops what they're doing and looks at her standing in the doorway.

"In your seats. Right this minute!"

Kids scramble to their desks. Ben doesn't move. He wants the frog back but is afraid to go after it. It's dead quiet.

Mrs. Tibbets walks into the room and slams a stack of books down on her desk. "I expect you to act like ladies and gentlemen when I'm out of the room," she says. "I have to walk all the way across the school to get back to you. Surely you can wait quietly for a minute." Then she notices Ben standing there. He isn't sure what to do. Frankie's in his seat, trying to look innocent.

"Ben," Mrs. Tibbets says, "that means you, too."

"I know, but—" Ben starts.

"But what? In your seat right now!"

There's nothing for Ben to do but head to his seat. He glances at Frankie, who's still holding on to the frog. Frankie isn't laughing now. In fact, his mouth is twisted into a scowl and his face is turning red. Everyone knows that Frankie has the frog. Everyone but the teacher.

Mrs. Tibbets turns to the whiteboard and starts to write on it. The room is quiet for all of ten seconds.

"Oh, gross!" Frankie yells, leaping from his chair. "It pooped on me!"

He drops the frog to the floor and holds his hands out like

they have toxic waste on them. Everyone shrieks and laughs.

"He pooped! He pooped!" Ryan squeals. He's up out of his seat, dancing around.

Mrs. Tibbets whirls around and glares at the class like they've all lost their minds. "What in heaven's name?"

"It pooped on my hands!" Frankie moans.

Then she sees the frog. It's just sitting there, like it belongs in science class. She walks over and looks down at it.

The classroom is dead quiet now.

Someone's going to die, Ben thinks. *And it will probably be me.*

"Frankie," Mrs. Tibbets says, "did you bring this into class?" She hasn't moved from where she's standing.

"No," Frankie says. His face is still red. "He did," he says, pointing at Ben. "He brought it into class and let it go, and I caught it so it wouldn't get hurt."

Ben feels sick to his stomach. He knows he's in hot water, but he's more worried about the frog. He never should have brought it into school. He's about to go grab the creature and is ready take whatever punishment he gets, but Mrs. Tibbets bends over and grasps the frog at its hips. The frog kicks its legs, and every single kid looks at Mrs. Tibbets in wonder. She cups it in her hand and strokes it underneath its chin.

"Ew!" someone says.

Mrs. Tibbets looks around at the class, and a mischievous smile spreads across her face. She kisses the frog.

"Ewww, gross!" Everyone is yelling, now, horrified and delighted.

When the class finally calms down, Mrs. Tibbets asks, "Who knows what this is?"

"A toad," says Frankie. "Duh."

Mrs. Tibbets doesn't say anything.

"No, it's not," Ben says.

Mrs. Tibbets looks at him quickly. "What is it, Ben?"

"It's a frog," he says.

"Frog, toad, what's the difference?" Frankie mutters. "It pooped on my hands."

Mrs. Tibbets ignores him. She walks toward Ben's desk. "And how do you know it's a frog and not a toad?"

"Well, by its color...and...and its skin," Ben says.

"What about its skin?"

"Well, it's smooth, and toads have bumpy skin. And its legs are longer than a toad's, I think. And toads have these bumps behind their ears that make this poison stuff."

"Parotid glands," Mrs. Tibbets says.

"I guess," Ben says.

Mrs. Tibbets nods. "You're right. It's a frog. Toads are a kind of frog, but they have certain characteristics that make them special, like you said. So, all toads are frogs, but not all frogs are toads. Do you know what kind of frog this is?"

Ben shakes his head.

"One that poops," Ryan says.

Mrs. Tibbets doesn't bat an eye. "All frogs poop. All living things poop. Pooping is part of living."

The kids all laugh. Mrs. Tibbets waits until the giggling dies down, then says, "This is a wood frog, and a very confused one, too. She's just come out, hoping to find a place to lay eggs and instead she's in science class."

Mrs. Tibbets holds the frog up to her face again and looks closely at it. Is she going to kiss it again?

"They have a funny call," she goes on. "They sound like ducks quacking."

"You mean it doesn't chirp or peep?" Ben asks. He's thinking about the sounds behind his house now. He's forgotten about being in trouble.

"No," she says. "Those are spring peepers." She looks at Ben with a wry look on her face, like she can't decide if she should smile or frown.

In that moment, Ben feels like she's looking right inside him.

"This frog is not very happy here," she says. Then she turns to Ryan. "Ryan, please run down to the cafeteria and ask for a jar to keep it in until Ben puts it back where it belongs."

"What do I do about the poop on my hands?" Frankie asks. Mrs. Tibbets gives him a dirty look, but Frankie doesn't seem to mind. Ben figures that Frankie's happy to have poop on his hands, if only so he can keep saying the word "poop."

"Ryan, go, and please be quick about it. Frankie, you may wash your hands."

Ryan hops out of his seat and bounces out the door, headed toward the cafeteria. Frankie leaves behind him. Ben sits at his seat, more confused than ever. He's waiting for Mrs. Tibbets to yell at him, but she just goes back to the front of the class. He's relieved, for sure, but also baffled. After what Mrs. Tibbets said, he's worried that he might have done something to hurt the frog.

Mrs. Tibbets is standing in the front of the classroom, trying to decide where to put the frog, when Mr. Nickelby, the principal, pushes Ryan through the door.

"Excuse me, Mrs. Tibbets, is this one of your students?" the principal asks stiffly. Everything about Mr. Nickelby is official, even his voice. He's always dressed very neatly in a suit and tie, like a businessman. Ben's only talked to him once, the day he enrolled in school last month. But he knows it's Mr. Nickelby's first year as a principal. And he looks young–tons younger than Mrs. Tibbets. Still, he's Mrs. Tibbets's boss, which seems completely weird to Ben.

Everybody in the room but the principal knows that Mrs. Tibbets is still holding the frog. The whole class is holding its breath. Mrs. Tibbets sighs. "Yes, Mr. Nickelby, this is one of my students."

"This young man was running down the hall. When I told him there was no reason to run, he explained that you had sent him on an emergency errand to the cafeteria."

The class looks at Mrs. Tibbets. She's holding the frog right out in plain sight.

"I did send him on an important errand. And I asked him to hurry. We need something for this." And she thrusts the frog out toward him like it's the most natural thing in the world to present to a principal.

Mr. Nickelby steps back. "A toad?" he says in his official principal voice.

"A FROG!" four or five students say all together, which doesn't help matters. Mr. Nickelby looks at the class like they're from Mars, and Mrs. Tibbets tries not to smile.

"Yes, Mr. Nickelby," she says. "My frog. It needs a home for the rest of the day, before it goes back where it belongs."

"Are you studying amphibians?" Mr. Nickelby asks.

"Not exactly. We're studying the water cycle, according to the curriculum. But it's early spring and frogs are around—and I really like them—so we're talking about frogs today."

Mr. Nickelby frowns. Mrs. Tibbets and the principal stand five feet apart, staring at each other. Finally Mr. Nickelby shakes his head and turns to Ryan.

"Young man, absolutely no running in the halls. Even when Mrs. Tibbets sends you on an errand."

"But she told me to hurry—" Ryan begins.

"No running, period." Mr. Nickelby gives Mrs. Tibbets one more hard look and heads out the door.

The class is silent, watching Mrs. Tibbets. She shakes her head. Ben has a lump in his throat. Mrs. Tibbets could have told Mr. Nickelby that he snuck the frog into class, but she didn't.

"Ryan," she says, "do you think you could please *walk* to the cafeteria and ask for a jar without getting any of us in any more trouble?"

"Sure, yeah," he says, and bounds out the door.

"No running!" Mrs. Tibbets yells after him as she heads back to her desk. She stops for a moment like she's thinking, then she opens the top drawer, puts the frog in, and shuts it.

"On with the water cycle!" she says, turning toward the board.

Everyone smiles. It's great to be in a science class with a frog in the drawer.

Ben's not sure exactly what just happened between Mrs. Tibbets and Mr. Nickelby, but it doesn't seem like they like each other very much. Did he get Mrs. Tibbets in trouble? His knee jiggles up and down as he thinks about it, and he presses his hand against his stomach, which is turning over and over like it has a life of its own. He feels horrible and excited at the same time. There's something very unusual about Mrs. Tibbets. Something he really likes.

At the end of the day, while everybody's getting ready to go home, Ben asks Mrs. Kutcher for permission to go back to the science room. He hopes Mrs. Tibbets is there. He wants the frog back.

Mrs. Tibbets is sitting at her desk. The frog is in a glass jar in front of her. Something feels sort of sad about Mrs. Tibbets, all alone in the room with the frog.

Ben takes in a deep breath, then lets it out all at once. "Mrs. Tibbets?"

She looks up. "Yes, Ben. Do you have a question about the homework?"

"It's about the frog." He waits a moment for her to say something. When she doesn't, he goes on. "I'm sorry I brought it in. And I shouldn't have had it out in class. Ryan wanted to see it, and it got away."

Mrs. Tibbets looks at him, then at the frog in the jar. "Where did you find it?" she asks.

"Out behind my house."

"In your backyard?"

"Not exactly." Ben hesitates, then the words pour out in a rush. "First I heard this chirping noise and when I followed it I came to this place where it's really wet. There were a lot of puddles, and a bunch of trees standing in the water. And then I heard the chirps again. I guessed it was frogs, or maybe toads—"

"Those were frogs. Spring peepers."

"How do you know?" Ben asks.

"I can't be sure without hearing them myself, but from the way you describe the place and the sound, I'd say it had to be peepers. I often go out to listen to them in the spring. I love being outdoors."

"Me too."

"My husband taught science, too. Biology. He was the one who really loved frogs."

"I like frogs," Ben says. "And lizards. At home, in Tucson, I had a terrarium with a gecko in it."

"Tucson. Is that where you moved from?"

Ben nods. "There was a wash near my house, where the river ran when it rained, and I found all sorts of great stuff there. Sometimes I went with my friend, Toby."

"I bet you miss it."

"Yeah, I do. It's...it's different here." Ben has already said more than he'd imagined he would. Mrs. Tibbets is the first person in Massachusetts who seems to have noticed anything about him. He likes Mrs. Kutcher all right, but she's never asked him about where he lived or what he likes.

Mrs. Tibbets picks up the jar and holds it out. "Well, Ben, I imagine that this frog feels the same way you do about missing her home. Why don't you take her and put her back where she belongs?"

Ben smiles. "Okay, I will. Sorry."

"That's all right. But no more frogs in school."

"Okay," Ben says.

"Unless I ask for them, of course." Mrs. Tibbets gives him a little wink.

Ben takes the jar. He's almost out of the classroom door when Mrs. Tibbets calls out, "Oh, Ben..."

He stops and turns back.

Mrs. Tibbets hesitates for a moment and then says, "The young man who used to help me around the yard has taken a full-time job at the landscape center. I have a big place, and I can't take care of it all by myself. Would you like to help me some Saturday? I have some nice woods and a pond on my land. When we get through working, maybe we could take a walk and see what kind of critters we can find there."

The word "critters" jumps out at Ben like an old friend—it's a word Mr. Tompkins always used. But Ben has never been to a teacher's house before. The whole thing seems a little strange.

"Sure," he says.

"Fine. Some Saturday, then. Whenever it stops raining."

"Okay," Ben says, and hurries down the hall carrying the glass jar with the toad inside.

He doesn't want to miss the bus. He's got a frog to deliver.

Chapter Five

That afternoon Ben carries the wood frog back to the place where he found it. He opens the jar and gently shakes the frog out onto a tuft of wet, brown grass. The frog sits where it landed, its neck moving in and out with its breath.

"Go ahead, fella." He prods it with his finger. "At least *you* get to go home."

He nudges the frog again and it leaps away. Ben squats down, looking around him. The rain has stopped. Finally. The clouds are passing quickly overhead and he can see patches of blue here and there. A breeze lifts the smell of the earth up into the air.

Behind him a shrill call rings out.

Eeep-eeeep.

Eeep-eeeep.

It's a spring peeper, the frog Mrs. Tibbets described. Ben is sure of it. He tries to figure out where the sound came from. There's no sign of anything moving. These frogs are well camouflaged. He sits and waits. He hears it again.

Eeeep-eeeep.

Eeeep-eeeeeep.

Nothing moves.

Then he sees it. He's been looking right at it. The frog, no bigger than his thumb, is perched on the end of a stubbly piece of grass. It's brownish green, the color of the grass itself. Across its back he sees the faint outline of a dark X that runs from both shoulders, the lines crossing on its back and ending near its legs.

Ben darts his hands out to scoop up the peeper. But before he gets anywhere near it, the frog leaps into the air and lands with a *plink* in a small pool near him, disappearing into the murky water filled with dark leaves and branches.

"Darn," Ben says. But he's smiling. Just seeing the frog feels like a little victory. He squats there for a while, trying to find another peeper, but has no luck. His legs are stiff, and it's getting dark. Finally Ben rises from his haunches and heads back to his house. The sounds of the chorus of spring peepers fill the heavy air.

Ben spends the weekend at home. He e-mails Lizardman, hoping to hear back from him right away, but he gets no response. His mother asks him if he wants to invite someone over to the house.

Ben shakes his head.

"Isn't there someone?" she asks.

"No, Mom. There isn't anyone."

On Monday morning Ben gets to school early. He pulls out his unfinished math homework, hoping to get it done before the last bell. Danny Martin, one of Frankie Mirley's friends, comes up to his desk and holds out an envelope. This is odd. He's never paid attention to Ben before.

"Here's an invitation to my birthday party," Danny blurts out. "It's at the skating rink Saturday morning. We're having pizza." He hands Ben the card and hurries back to his desk.

Ben looks at the invitation. He wants to go to the party. He likes pizza, and he'd like to be part of a group of kids. But he can't skate very well. And he's not sure why Danny invited him—it almost seems like he had to do it. His mom probably forced him to invite everyone in the class. Jenny flops into her seat in front of Ben. She sees him holding the card.

"Is that for Danny's party?"

"Yeah. Are you going?"

"I can't. I have a swim meet. Are you?"

"I don't know." Even though he's never talked to Jenny outside of school, he wishes she were going.

"It'll probably be fun," she says. "The pizza at the skating rink is really good."

Ben nods. The pizza is good. Maybe that's enough reason to go. Or maybe he could end up being friends with Danny.

At lunch Ben passes by the table where Danny and Frankie are sitting with a couple of other boys. There's no room for him at their end anyway. He chooses a half-empty table near the window and slides onto the bench.

"Hey, Ben!" Ryan rushes up and sits across from him. "Are you going to the party? Did you get an invitation?"

Ben shrugs.

"Are you going?" Ryan asks again.

"I don't know."

"Come on. If you go, I'll go. Then we'd have each other to hang around with."

Ben gives his milk carton a shake and pries open the top.

"I really, really hope you can go," Ryan says.

Ben feels kind of bad for Ryan. He's a nice enough kid in some ways, if only he weren't so hyper.

"Okay," Ben says, hoping he's not making a mistake. "I'll go."

A huge smile breaks out across Ryan's face. "Great. Cool. It'll be fun."

Ben smiles back. Maybe going to the party won't be so bad.

At the end of science class the next day, Mrs. Tibbets calls Ben up to the desk as the other students are leaving.

"Ben," she says, "do you remember what I asked you last week, about doing a little yard work around my house?"

Ben glances around to see if any of the other kids are still in the room. "Uh-huh. Sure."

"I was wondering if this Saturday morning might be a good time. You could help me for a while—I'll pay you, of course—and then if we have time, we could see what kind of little critters we might find in the woods. The toads are out, and the spring peepers are calling, even in the middle of the day. Maybe we could catch one."

"How? I tried the other day, but it hopped away before I could get close."

It seems like every part of the teacher's face crinkles up into a smile. "Oh, yes. They're very quick. Did you use a net?"

"No. I don't have a net. I just used my hands."

"Oh, a net makes it much easier!" she said. "I have a bunch of them. My husband must have left a dozen in our garage. I could certainly lend you one."

Hunting frogs with a net sounds like a good time, even if it means doing yard work for a teacher first.

"Okay," he says. He can't help feeling excited.

"I'd better call your parents to make sure it's all right. Would you give me your phone number?" She hands him a notebook.

"Okay, sure. That would be great." Ben writes down his phone number and hands the notebook back to her.

"I could pick you up at around ten in the morning," Mrs. Tibbets says. "And I can pay you five dollars an hour."

"Okay," Ben says. *Some extra spending money will be nice*, he thinks. *But catching some frogs will be even better.*

He heads down the hall to Mrs. Kutcher's class. He's thinking about nets and toads and frogs when all of a sudden he remembers Danny Martin's birthday party. He smacks himself on the head. *Dummy, dummy, dummy!* he says to himself. He'd forgotten all about it. He hasn't told Danny he's coming, but he has promised Ryan. Now he's told Mrs. Tibbets he'll help her on Saturday morning.

There's no way he can do both things.

Over the next two days Ben ignores the choice he has to make, hoping that somehow it will just go away. Or that something will happen to make clear what he should do. It makes his stomach turn just thinking about it.

Toads or ice skating?

Kids or science teacher?

Mrs. Tibbets calls and talks to his mother, like she said she would, and his mom thinks it's fine. "Maybe you'll learn to like Massachusetts," she says, "just like you love the desert."

Ben doubts that, but he's still excited about exploring the woods. He doesn't even mind the thought of a little yard work. How hard can it be?

Danny's party is still a problem, though. He hasn't shown his parents the invitation, but part of him would like to go to the skating rink. Everyone will be there. He did tell Ryan he would go. And he hates feeling left out—which is all he's felt ever since he moved.

But then there are the frogs.

He can't tell anyone else about working at Mrs. Tibbets's. Other kids would think he was crazy, working for a teacher and chasing frogs instead of going to a skating party.

Ben can almost hear the peepers calling. He can't get them out of his mind. He remembers the one that got away. It's going to be hard to catch a peeper. They're fast, and they're hard to find in the first place. He just wants to hold one for a minute, and feel it in his hands.

By lunchtime on Friday Ben still hasn't made up his mind about Saturday. But he's thinking he should go to the skating rink since he was invited to the party first and he promised Ryan he'd go. As he heads to the lunch table, he sees Danny already sitting there with no one beside him. *Maybe I should try being friends,* Ben thinks. *He's nice when Frankie's not around.* "Hi, Danny."

"Hey, Ben. Want to trade your fries for my pudding?"

"Sure," Ben says. He hates banana pudding and he really wants his french fries, but he agrees. He's about to hand over the french fries when Frankie shows up and slides in on the other side of Danny.

"Hey, Danny, trade you half my fries for your pudding," Frankie says.

Danny looks at Frankie, glances back at Ben, then says, "Sure, yeah, great."

Ben feels like a total idiot, sitting there holding a handful of fries.

Danny starts talking to Frankie as if Ben isn't there. They laugh and joke, and Ben sits looking at his plate, still holding the limp fries.

Forget it, he thinks. *I don't want to go to your stupid party.*

When Ben and Agatha get home from school, their mother is waiting for them in the kitchen. She puts some snacks on the table and sits down. “Ben,” she says, “I’m a little confused.”

“About what?” Ben asks.

“I got a phone call from Danny Martin’s mother today. Do you know who he is?”

“Uh-huh.”

“She asked if you were coming to his birthday party tomorrow. Did you get an invitation?”

“Yeah.”

“Why didn’t you tell me?”

“I guess I forgot.”

“Don’t you want to go?”

Ben shrugs. “No. I’m going to Mrs. Tibbets’s house, remember?”

“But surely Mrs. Tibbets would understand. She wouldn’t want you to miss a birthday party. Don’t you think you’d have fun? You might make some new friends.”

Ben is sick of hearing about new friends. “I don’t care about that,” he says. “I told Mrs. Tibbets I was coming and I want to go there.”

His mother gets up and goes to the refrigerator. Without a word she takes out a bunch of broccoli and some mushrooms and goes over to the kitchen counter. She doesn’t mention the party again.

But his dad does. After dinner he tries to talk Ben into going.

"Won't the birthday boy be disappointed? Aren't kids going to miss you?" his father asks. "The frogs can wait."

Ben shakes his head. "No one cares if I come or not."

"No one? Absolutely no one? No one on the planet?" His father pokes him in the ribs. It makes Ben mad.

"No one!" Ben says, but even as he says it, he wonders what Ryan will do when he shows up at the party and sees that Ben isn't there.

His father frowns and scratches his head. He always scratches his head when he doesn't know what to do. Ben sometimes teases him about it, but not tonight. "It's your life, bud," his dad says. "But you need to make some friends here. We're not moving."

"I wish we would."

His father reaches out, wraps his arm around Ben's head, and pulls it in close to his chest. Before Ben can twist out of his grasp, his dad gives his head a vigorous rubbing with his knuckles.

"I know you do, Ben," his father says. "But we're not moving. I know it's hard, and I wish we could bring all your friends and all your critters and even a cactus or two here. But we can't. All you can do is try and make friends here."

"But I don't want to!" Ben feels tears welling up in his eyes. "I don't like the kids here. They're idiots! I hate it here.

And I still don't even have my box of things from my room."

His father gives Ben's head one last rub and hugs him closer. "Well, idiots are everywhere. Even in Tucson. But there are good guys, too. Even in Massachusetts. You've got to hang in there a little longer. And hey, if you're not going to the birthday party, at least you'll see some critters tomorrow with your science teacher."

Chapter Six

Ben opens the front door the moment the bell rings. His mom comes up behind him in the doorway. Mrs. Tibbets is dressed in old jeans, a brown canvas jacket, and the same leather hiking boots she wears at school. "Hello, Ben. And you must be Mrs. Moroney. I'm Gloria Tibbets." She holds out her hand.

"I'm so happy you called," his mom says as she shakes the teacher's hand. "Would you like me to pick him up?"

"Oh, no, no," the teacher says. "I'll bring him back right after we get the work done and have a bite to eat."

Mrs. Tibbets's car is a beat-up old station wagon. Ben has trouble getting the passenger door open until Mrs. Tibbets opens it from the inside.

"Darn door," she says. "I don't use it much."

Inside, the car is like a storage shed that hasn't been

cleaned out for a long time. The backseat is folded down to make more room for all the stacked-up boxes and plastic containers. Boots and raincoats are piled on top of the boxes. Spades and shovels and nets like the ones used for hauling in fish after they're caught have been thrown in anywhere they'll fit. Mrs. Tibbets gathers the books and papers from the passenger seat and crams them between two boxes in the back.

"There. This'll do for now," she says, "but I need to clean this car out in the worst way. It's worse than my desk. Worse than my brain." She laughs an easy, comfortable laugh.

Ben doesn't mind the mess. He looks in the backseat, remembering Mr. Tompkins at the Desert Museum and all the equipment the people there used. While he's looking, Mrs. Tibbets keeps talking.

"I really appreciate your help today. I know kids don't like to give up their Saturdays. But I have to move some things around in the yard, and I just can't do it all by myself. You'll see. Hopefully no one will bother us and we can get some work done."

Mrs. Tibbets checks the rearview mirror and backs out of his driveway. "You can open the window if you want."

Ben rolls the window down. The air is warm and the sun is shining. There aren't any leaves on the trees yet, but it feels like things are coming back to life. He looks over at Mrs. Tibbets as she drives. He's never ridden in a teacher's car before, let alone been to a teacher's house.

"Will your husband be there to help, too?" he asks.

Mrs. Tibbets keeps her eyes on the road. "My husband died last year, so I'm afraid he won't be much help today. If he could, he would. He loved being outdoors."

Ben swallows. He feels horrible. He should have figured that out by himself. That's why she left school for a while! He fumbles for something to say, but Mrs. Tibbets keeps talking.

"I really do need help—that's why I asked. And it sounds like you enjoy being outside."

Ben nods. "In Tucson, I spent a lot of time outdoors. A lot by myself. And with my friend, Toby."

It's Mrs. Tibbets's turn to nod. It strikes Ben that they're both talking about someone they've lost, though moving away from your best friend is nothing like losing someone you're married to. He sneaks another look at Mrs. Tibbets. Maybe that's why her eyes look sad, even when she laughs. She keeps looking straight ahead. He can't think of anything else to say.

"You live pretty close to me as the crow flies," Mrs. Tibbets says. "Those woods behind your house connect to the woods behind mine, although it would be hard to find your way through. But I have a lot of frogs on my property, too. Several different kinds."

It's better when she's doing all the talking, Ben thinks.

She goes on. "American toads will be coming out pretty soon. And even some spadefoots."

"Spadefoots?" Ben has heard of spadefoots, but he doesn't know much about them.

"Right," Mrs. Tibbets says. "Eastern spadefoots. They're very rare around here. This is as far north as they get. But we've got some." She turns off the main road onto a winding street. They drive past a wooded lot with no houses and then pull into a driveway.

He peers out the car window. The little house is set way back from the street, but there's hardly any lawn. Instead, there are bushes and trees and large flowerbeds covered with straw. The car comes to a stop and Ben gets out. He sees a one-car garage to his left, connected to the house by a covered walkway. A couple of bare, gnarled trees loom over the front porch.

"Looks like a pretty old house," Ben says.

"The oldest part is one hundred and forty years old," Mrs. Tibbets says. "Almost older than me."

Ben looks at her.

"That's a joke," Mrs. Tibbets says. "Come around back and I'll show you what to do."

They walk to the back of the house. It faces south, so the morning sun is reflecting off the windowpanes. The backyard stretches out into a meadow of tall, uncut, tawny grass, with woods at the far end. Small trees and bushes are arranged in rough lines over part of the meadow. Just beyond the garage, Ben sees what looks like a fenced-in vegetable garden with piles of brush and weeds heaped nearby. Off to the left, a hill rises steeply with a bare outcropping of rocks crowning its top.

It looks like a great place to explore.

As if reading his mind, Mrs. Tibbets says, "Want to look around a bit before we get to work?"

"Sure." He follows his teacher out to the middle of the field, and they stop and stand by the rows of bushes.

"These are blueberries," Mrs. Tibbets says, fingering one of the bare branches. "The birds get most of them."

"Is this all your land?" Ben asks.

"Yes," she says. "Well, mine and my sister-in-law's."

Ben looks back at the house. There's a big toolshed behind the garage. "Is this a farm or something?" he asks.

"It was, once upon a time. My husband's father farmed it, and his father did, too. But they weren't serious farmers. It's hard to farm here because the soil is very rocky. A lot of the fields have gone back to woods now. Anyway, Thomas inherited the house and the land right around it—it's where he grew up. He loved it here."

Ben notices a little lean-to against the toolshed. A large cage up on legs sits under the lean-to roof. It looks like a rabbit hutch.

"What's that?" he asks, pointing.

Mrs. Tibbets shakes her head and says, "It's a snake cage."

Ben's ears perk up. "Are there snakes in there?"

"Yes. My husband kept them."

"What kind?"

"It doesn't matter," Mrs. Tibbets said. "You must leave them alone and not go near them."

"But are they—?"

"I'm dead serious. Don't go near the cage. Do you understand me?"

Ben nods. He can tell she doesn't want to talk about it anymore. It only makes him more curious.

"Let's get to work," Mrs. Tibbets says, "so we'll have time later to look for the frogs." Mrs. Tibbets opens the door of the toolshed. "Wait here. I need to get a few things."

Ben can't help staring at the cages. What could be in there?

Mrs. Tibbets hands Ben a rake and a big plastic tarp and leads him around to a large flowerbed on the side of the house away from the garage. She instructs him to rake the leaves out of the bed and pile them up on the tarp, then leaves him there to work in the sun. Soon he's sweating. Just as he's finishing with the beds, she reappears and points out a pile of fallen branches. "I want you to drag these limbs out to the back part of the field. Cover for animals," she says. "A place they can hide from hawks."

Ben can't remember the last time he worked this hard, but the morning goes by quickly. When he's moved all the branches out to the field, he sits on a rock wall and enjoys the sun for a minute. He's still breathing heavily, but a light breeze cools his face. Now that he's still, he can hear birds singing.

"All done?" Mrs. Tibbets calls. She has something that looks like deflated inner tubes draped over her shoulders.

"I think so," Ben answers.

"Let's go for a walk, then," she says and holds up a really long pair of boots. "We'll take these hip waders in case we want to wade in some muck."

Ben has seen pictures of boots like these, but he's never worn any. He puts a pair over his shoulder and follows Mrs. Tibbets. She stops at the edge of the woods and points to an opening in the trees.

"My husband made this trail years ago. It loops back around through the woods in a big circle and comes out near the garage," she says, then heads off down the trail at a quick pace. Before Ben knows it, Mrs. Tibbets is down the path, almost twenty yards ahead of him.

Ben struggles along, lugging the big boots, following the faint trail. He pushes past a tangle of briars and fallen tree branches and nearly steps on Mrs. Tibbets, who is kneeling by a log. She lifts it up slightly.

"Look!" she says.

Ben squats beside her. Huddled under the log is a little squirmy thing a couple of inches long, with legs and a tail. It has yellow spots up and down its back. Ben gets down on his knees right by Mrs. Tibbets.

"What is it?"

"A yellow spotted salamander. It's just waking up now."

Ben is impressed. "How'd you know it was there?"

"Well, I wasn't sure. But they like moist places, and they usually burrow around roots, so I made an educated guess."

She seems to know something about everything on this trail. She brushes back leaves and shows him where tiny white wildflowers called bloodroot are already blooming. She stops in front of a tree and breaks off a twig. "Chew on the end of it," she says.

Ben bites down on the twig and his mouth fills with a sudden sweetness. "It tastes sort of minty."

"Black birch," Mrs. Tibbets says. "People used it to make root beer. It's also got a natural painkiller in it."

Ben had never thought of root beer coming from an actual plant before. Mrs. Tibbets heads farther down the trail and he runs to keep up.

When the path skirts a swampy area, Ben sees the bright green shoots of a plant sticking up out of the marshy ground, like the ones behind his house. "What's that?" he asks.

"Skunk cabbage."

"Why do they call it that?"

"Why do you think?" she asks.

"Because skunks eat it?"

"No." She laughs. "Because if you break the leaves, the smell is just horrible. Like a skunk. Want me to pick some for you to sample?"

"No thanks," Ben says. "I'll take your word for it."

"Try to stay right behind me on the trail," Mrs. Tibbets advises. "There are lots of plants and critters here that wouldn't appreciate being squashed by our big feet!"

Ben follows her, stopping to marvel at everything she points out. This isn't the Sonoran Desert, of course, but it is about a hundred times more interesting than he had expected.

"You getting tired?" Mrs. Tibbets looks back at him. "We've been at it for a while. We're looping back toward the house now."

Ben shakes his head. He's lost track of time.

"Well, we're nearly there. Just beyond those red maples." She skirts around a clump of trees and stops in a clearing in front of a pool of water about twenty feet across. The sun is glinting on the water.

"Here it is," she says.

"Here's what?"

"Where the spadefoots will be. In a month or so."

"It just looks like a big puddle."

"It is. A special puddle called a vernal pool. Vernal means spring. The pool is only here in the spring, but a lot of things depend on it to live—wood frogs, salamanders, fairy shrimp."

"Shrimp?

"Fairy shrimp. Tiny crustaceans about an inch long. And spadefoots. They only breed on one night—the rainiest night in April—and then they're gone."

"Where?"

"Back underground. They're very private and only come out at night. The night they breed is about the only chance you have to see them. One night a year—and that's it! They're almost impossible to find. You can hear them, though, on that night."

"Really?"

"Oh yes, they make quite a racket."

She sits down on a large rock by the pool and takes off her shoes, then pulls on the wading boots. Ben does the same. They are way too big for him, and when he stands up he loses his balance. "Aaaah!" he says, trying not to fall over, but he ends up sprawling in the wet muck at the edge of the pool. His hands are muddy, his forearms wet, and a rich, funky smell comes up from the muck. He tries to get up, but it's hard in the boots. He's on his hands and knees and feels stupid. He looks up at Mrs. Tibbets. She's laughing.

"Oh, for Pete's sake," she says. "It's not a swimming pool!"

Something about the way she says it makes Ben laugh, too. She reaches down a hand and pulls him up. His arms are smeared with wet mud. He rubs them on the front of his jacket.

"You look like the Creature from the Black Lagoon," Mrs. Tibbets says. "Your mother will kill me." She hands him a bandanna and he wipes the mud off his fingers.

"At least my feet are dry," he says.

Mrs. Tibbets laughs again and wades out to the middle of the pool. Ben starts to follow. "Try not to stir things up," she says. She inches along, bending down and peering into the murky water, and Ben follows behind, feeling the cool of the water through the boots.

Ben can't figure out what she's doing. "Do you see anything?" he asks.

She doesn't answer. After several minutes she says, "Look! Over here!"

Ben wades over, and she points at a gooey-looking blob floating in the pond. Inside the clear goo are hundreds of little black dots.

"What is it?"

"Wood frog eggs."

"Like the one I caught?"

"Who knows? Maybe she's the one that laid them."

"What are the black dots?"

"The eggs."

"But there must be a thousand of them!"

"About that many," Mrs. Tibbets says. "Most of them won't make it."

"Why not?"

"Because they taste soooooo good! Yum yum. At least to snakes."

Ben stares at the mass of eggs. "Cool," he says. He shakes

his head at himself. That sounded more like what Ryan would say.

"Very cool," Mrs. Tibbets answers. "And the spadefoots are even cooler. They're my favorite." She stands up and rubs her back, stiff from leaning over.

They wade out of the mucky water and put their shoes back on. It feels good to be back in sneakers. They sit on the rock for a little while. The sun warms Ben's back. "It's nice here," he says.

"Yes. Very nice." Without another word, Mrs. Tibbets gets up and heads down the path toward the house. "Let's get some lunch," she calls back to him, "then I'll pay you and take you home."

Ben had forgotten all about the money. He'd forgotten all about everything. Even the birthday party. "Okay," he says happily, hurrying to catch up, toting the wet boots over his shoulder.

As they come to the side of the house by the garage, a fancy car pulls in the driveway and a woman wearing an expensive-looking coat gets out. Her hair is bright red.

"Oh for Pete's sake," Mrs. Tibbets mutters. "I wonder what she wants. Um, Ben, why don't you find something to do in the backyard for a couple of minutes while I talk to her."

Ben looks at Mrs. Tibbets.

"It's just Tabitha, my sister-in-law," she says with a frown on her face. “Go on. It won’t take long. There’s no reason for you to have to talk to her.” She takes Ben’s boots and walks across the yard.

Ben is happy for an excuse not to meet the redheaded woman. He can tell by the look on Mrs. Tibbets’s face that her sister-in-law isn’t someone he really wants to meet. He’s almost to the walkway between the house and garage when he hears their voices getting louder. At first he can’t really hear their words, but they both sound annoyed. He retraces his steps and stands behind the shrubs at the corner of the house.

“I know how you feel, Gloria, but it’s really my decision.” Ben can tell that it’s the redheaded woman speaking. The words sound brittle, like they might break when they come out of her mouth.

“It’s not what Thomas would have wanted,” Mrs. Tibbets says.

“I know very well what he wanted. He asked me to wait a year.”

“He said not to do anything for at *least* a year,” Mrs. Tibbets says. “I don’t think he intended for you to sell. Not like this, anyway. And although you don’t seem to care what I think, it’s certainly not what I want.”

Ben feels sneaky, but he can’t help listening. It’s weird. Even though he doesn’t know Mrs. Tibbets all that well, something about her sharp-tongued sister-in-law alarms him.

"Really, Gloria," the other woman snaps. "You're being pigheaded. It's best for both of us."

"Fifteen houses jammed up next to mine is not my idea of what's best for me. It won't be the same. And Thomas loved this land as it was—not with roads and houses."

"Oh, you act like they're going to put a nuclear waste dump here or something!" Tabitha's voice sounds agitated now.

"I could stop this," Mrs. Tibbets says.

"Don't you dare start with that again," the other woman snaps, her voice rising.

"I could, though."

"If you call the state about that, I'll just...I'll...," the woman sputters. "Really, Gloria. This is not your decision, and anyway you need the money more than I do. Look at the house. It needs painting—"

"I know very well what it needs."

"I'm only trying to help."

"It's help I don't really want, Tabitha."

"Ohhh, it's no use trying to reason with you. You are so, so stubborn!"

"No more than you," Mrs. Tibbets says.

There's a pause. Ben can feel his heart beating so loudly he's afraid they're both going to hear it. The other woman speaks again. "In the end, it's my decision. Legally this is my land, and I'm going to get the best price I can for it. You'll get your share as Tom requested in his will, and then you can decide what you want to do with it. And remember, I don't legally owe you any more than that—I'm just honoring what my brother wanted."

Ben can barely hear his teacher's response. "Well, whatever you're going to do, you're going to do."

"I wish you wouldn't be like this."

"I'm afraid it's just the way I am. Come inside and I'll see if I can find the papers."

Ben hears the front door close. Mrs. Tibbets seems to have forgotten about him. He's breathing hard, like he was in the argument himself. He wanders around back. He thinks about exploring the woods again, but he doesn't want to get too far away from the house, in case Mrs. Tibbets comes looking for him. He opens the door of the toolshed a crack and peers inside. Nothing but garden tools and a big pile of empty plant containers.

Outside again, he wanders over to the back of the shed. The cage underneath the lean-to is partially hidden in the shadows. He edges closer. It's made of wood and wire tightly woven into half-inch squares. A plywood wall marks off a small corner of the cage. It looks like some kind of shelter area with a small entrance. He tries to peer into the entrance, but it's just too dark.

Don't go near the cage, Mrs. Tibbets had said.

What kind of snakes are in there? Ben shakes the cage a

little to see if he can get anything to come out. There's no movement, and maybe there's nothing in there at all. But then why did Mrs. Tibbets tell him to stay away?

Ben looks around on the ground and finds a skinny stick. He pushes the stick through the wire and into the hole in the nesting area. He twists and wiggles it gently inside the hole.

Ben hears a car motor start up on the other side of the garage. He pulls the stick out and flings it on the ground. He runs around the side of the house and smack into Mrs. Tibbets, almost knocking her over.

"Oh!" she says.

"Sorry," says Ben.

"What were you doing back there?" Mrs. Tibbets says. Her voice is tense.

"I was just walking around, looking at stuff," Ben says. It's a horrible answer.

"You weren't bothering the snakes, were you?"

Ben shakes his head "No. I wasn't." He feels bad about lying. But nothing happened and he doesn't want her to be mad at him.

"You have to promise," Mrs. Tibbets says. "Don't go near the cage." She puts her hand to her chest, like she's trying to calm down. She lets out a breath. "I'm sorry if I yelled. But it's very important. They're not to be disturbed. Do you understand?"

Ben nods. Mrs. Tibbets rubs her forehead, then without a

word she turns and heads toward the house. Ben follows her through the back door into the kitchen.

It's a small room, with a table just big enough for two chairs. A cardboard box overflowing with papers and files takes up most of the surface of the table, and two more boxes just like it are sitting on the floor.

"Sorry about all the mess," Mrs. Tibbets says, not looking at him. "I was just going through some old things." She picks up one of the boxes and carries it out to some other room.

Ben's heart is still pounding from his teacher's scolding. He looks at the box on the table. Balanced on top is a stack of black-and-white photographs. He sits in one of the chairs and leans in for a better look. Some of the pictures are yellowed and curled up on the edges. He guesses they're old. Probably as old as the photos in his grandmother's family album. Ben listens for the sound of Mrs. Tibbets's footsteps. He only hears a faint scraping in the back of the house. He takes a chance and flips through a few of the pictures: groups of people—relatives, probably—posing at holiday time or standing by the beach or leaning against old cars. Then one of a boy and a girl catches his eye.

The boy looks like he's about eight years old—younger than Ben is now—and the girl looks around six. They're sitting on a large rock, squinting into the sun. The boy, his face all scrunched up, is holding something away from himself, like he's not sure he really wants to touch it. Ben can't tell if he's laughing or upset. Maybe both. He peers at the object in the boy's hands. It looks like some sort of toad. The girl has something, too. Her long, curly hair hangs down over her shoulders, but Ben can see that she's holding an even fatter toad under her chin. She's laughing. He flips over the picture and sees someone has written, in a kid's scrawl, "Tom, me, and the Overtoad." He looks at it again. He doesn't notice when Mrs. Tibbets comes back in the room.

"That's Thomas, my husband."

Startled, Ben drops the photo on the table. "W-who's the girl?" he asks.

"It looks like Tabitha," she says, hurrying to the refrigerator. "How does chicken salad sound to you?'

"Fine," says Ben.

Neither of them says much during lunch. *Maybe I should have gone to the birthday party,* Ben thinks. *The walk in the woods was fun, but now everything feels strange.*

"You did good work today," Mrs. Tibbets says, handing him an envelope.

Ben peers inside. Fifteen dollars. "That's too much," he says.

"No it's not. It's what you earned."

"Okay." Ben folds the envelope and puts it in his pocket. "Thanks."

With barely another word Mrs. Tibbets stacks the lunch dishes in the kitchen sink and leads him through the house, out the front door, and back to the car. As she drives him home she hums to herself, letting her voice fill the space where there's no talking. When she stops the car in front of his house, Ben opens the car door to climb out.

"Ben?"

"Yes?"

"I'm sorry I yelled at you about the cage."

"It's okay."

"There are a couple of snakes in that cage. I shouldn't have them there, really. My husband rescued them from an area being developed, and he was looking for a nature center that might take them. He was a real herpetologist. The things everyone else was afraid of, he loved. This was just before he died—it was very sudden. I shouldn't have kept them. I know I need to find a place for them, I just haven't gotten around to doing it."

"What kind of snakes?" he asks.

She ignores his question. "You should never bother them. Do you understand?"

Ben nods again.

"So, enough of that," Mrs. Tibbets says. "Thanks for coming. I really needed your help."

Ben smiles. He's glad she's not mad anymore. He hates it when adults are angry—he never knows what to do or say. "It's okay. Thanks for everything."

"No, thank *you.* And maybe we could look for those spadefoot toads when we get a good rain."

"Cool!" he says. *Where'd that come from?* he wonders. Ryan again.

"Cool," Mrs. Tibbets repeats. It sounds funny coming from her. Funny, but nice.

Chapter Seven

On Monday morning everyone's talking about Danny's party. It seems like the whole school was there. Ryan comes up to Ben right before the beginning of reading.

"Why weren't you there?" Ryan asks. "You said you were coming."

"I had to do something else," Ben says.

"You promised!"

"I didn't exactly promise. I just had to go somewhere else."

"Where?"

Ben didn't answer. He wished Ryan would give up and go away.

"Where'd you have to go that was so important? You said you were coming to the party."

"I had to do some work for Mrs. Tibbets."

"Mrs. Tibbets?" Ryan frowns. "Mrs. Tibbets, the *teacher?*"

"Uh-huh."

"What kind of work?"

"Just yard work."

"You worked for a teacher?"

"What's wrong with that? She paid me more than I ever made for yard work before. Anyway, she'd already talked with my mom and I couldn't get out of it."

That seems to satisfy Ryan. He probably still feels hurt, but he goes back to his desk without asking any more questions. Ben is relieved. Ryan will forget all about Danny's party in a day or two and things will go back to normal.

At lunch Ben sits down at a table across from Jenny. Before he can even take a bite of his pizza, though, Frankie comes over with his tray and glares at him.

"You missed the party so you could go to Mrs. Tibbets's house?" he says, making it sound like the dumbest thing he's ever heard of.

Ben shrugs. Ryan sure didn't waste any time letting everyone know. So much for things getting back to normal.

"Mrs. Tibbets is a loser," Frankie says. "What were you doing at her house?"

Everyone at the table—even Jenny—is staring at Ben. He feels his face turning red. "She's okay," he mumbles. That's not what he wants to say. But who's going to admit that he likes a teacher and would rather be with her than skating with kids his own age?

"Yeah, right," Frankie snorts. "She's okay, if you like crummy teachers. She's old. And she's wacko."

"She is not. She knows a lot," says Ben. "She knows a lot about science."

"Then why's she teaching in that little room?" Frankie fires back. "It isn't even a real science room. They had to put her somewhere because they can't fire her. And if she's so great, how come Mr. Nickelby is always checking on what she's doing?"

At first Ben doesn't know what he's talking about. But then he remembers the principal coming in the room and confronting Mrs. Tibbets. And he remembers Mrs. Tibbets sticking the frog in the principal's face.

Frankie looks at him in disgust. "Well, Danny sure is mad. Instead of coming to his birthday party, you go and hang out with some old teacher." He rolls his eyes and heads toward another table.

Jenny takes a bite of her sandwich. "If you ask me," she says with her mouth full, "Frankie's the one who's a wacko."

A couple of kids laugh. Ben looks up and smiles at her. It won't solve his problems with Frankie. But it sure helps to have *someone* on his side.

On the playground, Ben sits with his back against the brick wall, watching Frankie and Danny and a bunch of other boys playing basketball. Since Ben is big, kids are always asking him to play, but he doesn't really like basketball. Especially not today. He knows he should say something to Danny about the party, but it's not going to be easy. As they all come up the walk after the bell, Ben catches up with him.

"Hey, Danny, I'm sorry I wasn't able to come to your party. I'm sorry I—"

"Who cares?" Danny says, pushing past.

Ben stands there on the walk as other kids rush around him.

That evening, right after dinner, Ben asks his mother if he can call Toby. He wants to talk to somebody. Especially somebody who doesn't live in Massachusetts.

Toby answers the phone after only one ring. Ben can hear laughing and yelling in the background.

"Hello?" Toby shouts.

"Toby, it's me. Ben. Snakeman."

"Knock it off for a minute, guys!" Toby says away from the

phone. "I'm trying to talk here." Ben hears some scuffling, then Toby's voice again. "Hey, Ben. How are you?"

"Okay," Ben says.

Another round of loud laughing. "You should be here now!" Toby yells. "Everybody's eating dinner here."

Ben feels sick. "Great," he says. "Who's there?"

"Josh and Bill. Oh, and Larry."

"Larry? Larry Dunstan?"

"Yeah. Too bad you're not here."

"But...Larry's such a jerk." Ben feels terrible the moment he says this, but Larry had always driven him and Toby crazy.

"No, he's okay now. We're on the same soccer team."

"You're playing soccer?" Ben asks. Toby's never played soccer before.

"Yeah, we had a practice this afternoon, and we're all on the same team. So my mom just brought us back here to eat."

Ben hears another shriek in the background. His heart drops through his shoes. "How's Lenny?" he asks.

"Okay. Eating and sleeping."

Ben has had enough. "Fine," he says. "I guess I gotta go now."

"Me too. Talk to you later."

Ben listens to the phone click. "Everything stinks," he says to himself. "Absolutely everything."

He puts on his raincoat and takes a flashlight from the drawer in the kitchen.

His mother is at the kitchen table working on some papers. She looks up.

"Where are you going?"

"I just want to go out for a little while. In the back."

His mother looks at him for a long moment. "Okay," she says finally. "Don't go out for too long. And don't go too far away."

He slips out the back door and down the steps.

The porch light shines out across the backyard. A fine mist is falling—Ben can barely feel it. It makes the air foggy and damp. He remembers someone saying that fog is just a cloud, low to the ground. He likes the idea of walking through a cloud. The light in the sky is fading, but it's not quite dark yet. He heads down the path through the woods, hardly aware of where he's going.

I don't have a single good friend in Massachusetts, he thinks.

My best friend is hanging out with a kid I can't stand.

Everybody thinks I'm an idiot for going to a teacher's house.

He walks until he reaches the marsh, where the trees open up a little and there's more light from the gray evening sky.

They're already calling.

Ben stands with his flashlight off, the sound of his breathing loud under his hood. His mind is racing in a million different directions.

Peep-peep. Peep-peep.

Peep-peep. Peep-peep.

He takes a deep breath, lets it out, and listens. There are three or four calling, but it's hard to pinpoint exactly where the calls are coming from. The voices seem to hover in the air, filling the space over the marsh—almost more of a presence than a sound.

More join in. They seem to call and answer each other, get closer and closer together in time, then join, calling together. Then they separate again, singing back and forth. Again and again.

Ben stands, transfixed, feeling like he's in a trance.

He's in the middle of a huge living machine—a pulsing thing. The peeps are the heartbeat or motor.

The engine of life.

It surrounds him, calling out louder and louder. He forgets all about school and Frankie Mirley and Tucson and Toby.

A peeper sings close to his foot, at the edge of a small pool of water. Ben bends over carefully, without turning on the flashlight, and sits back on his heels. Waiting. His hands and feet are getting cold. But he doesn't move. The soft gray world is filled with the sound of the peepers. And then he hears a trill above the other sounds. It must be the American toads calling out, too, high and steady—a backdrop for his nearby peeper's song.

He's afraid to turn on the flashlight, afraid he'll stop the music, afraid he might somehow stop the world. He strains to see in the growing darkness, trying to make out the little creature that is only inches away from him. It's no good, though. He can't see it.

Finally he points the flashlight toward the spot the sound seems to be coming from and switches it on. A circle of bright white light shines on a tuft of grass.

The singing continues. He keeps looking but he can't see the peeper. The singing stops. Did it get away? He stares harder.

Then he sees it, clinging with its tiny toes to a broad blade of grass. Its eyes sparkle in the light; life pulses in its pale throat. Ben grips the flashlight in one hand, holding his breath. The peeper stays where it is. With his other hand Ben reaches out, slowly, carefully, trying to get closer. Then he grabs for it.

"Gotcha!" he says. He can feel its hind legs pushing hard against his palm. He drops the flashlight so he can cup the frog in both hands, and the beam of the flashlight shoots up into the darkening sky. He really can't see what he's doing, but he manages to get a hold of the peeper behind the hips so that he has it firmly but gently between his thumb and finger. Then he picks up the flashlight and trains the light on the frog. The peeper has stopped struggling and seems to have calmed down. Its back legs are hanging down; its throat is moving in and out.

And then, for a minute or two, or maybe ten—he doesn't know how long—Ben studies the frog, holding it carefully between his fingers. He thinks about taking it to school.

"Be-en! Be-en!" His mother's voice calls out through the night, over the sound of the frogs and toads. Over the pounding of his heart.

He opens his hand. For a moment the peeper just sits on his palm. Then it springs out of his hand, out of the circle of light, back into the night.

Ben turns the flashlight off, stands up, and listens.

"Be-en!"

"Coming!" he calls, and he starts back. He doesn't turn the flashlight on. He knows his way home.

Chapter Eight

Ben is sitting in class the next morning, and Mrs. Kutcher is writing assignments on the board. The spelling words are there to be copied, but Ben's not interested. Last night his mother found one of his favorite books, *Amphibians of the World,* when she was unpacking one of the boxes in his sister's room. Ben hugged it to his chest like a lost friend, then stayed up late reading and studying the photographs.

He opens the book on his lap and leafs through the pages again. Spelling can wait. He turns to the section on frogs and toads in Costa Rica and finds the picture of the golden toad, whose skin is an absolutely brilliant golden orange. The book says the golden toad hasn't been seen for more than a decade. Scientists think it's extinct. Frogs are disappearing all over the world.

Ben starts to draw a picture of the golden toad. His colored pencils are dull, so he gets up to sharpen them. Ryan follows him to the sharpener.

"Ben," Ryan whispers. "Hey, Ben!"

"Yeah?"

"This is for you!" Ryan hands him an envelope. Ben's name is on the front, written carefully in large block letters.

"You can open it now, but be kind of quiet!" Ryan says. He's hopping back and forth from one foot to another, doing his crazy dance, waiting. Ben shrugs and opens the envelope. The card inside is in the shape of a party hat.

"I'm having my own party, like Danny's but different. It's in a month. I'm giving you the invitation early so you can make sure to come."

"Okay," says Ben.

"It'll be cool. We're planning all this fun stuff. We have to have it on Thursday because my mom works on the weekend. My sister'll be there, but she promised not to bother us, and my mom says we can order pizza..." Ryan pauses for a quick breath, then the words keep coming. "We'll have games and a movie. What movies do you like? What—"

"Anything's fine," says Ben. The party's a month away, and Ryan's already going crazy.

"My mom says maybe your mom should call, so we can get everything set."

"Okay." Ben finishes sharpening his colored pencils and heads for his desk. Ryan grabs his sleeve.

"She should call today, and I—"

"Ryan, calm down. I got your invitation. I'm coming! My mom doesn't need to call."

"Okay, yeah, I know. I just want to make sure because it'll be fun. Okay?"

"Okay, okay."

Ryan turns and hops back to his desk. He careens into his seat, knocking his books onto the floor.

Mrs. Kutcher looks up. "Ryan," she says, "please keep it down. Others are working."

"Sure," he says. "Sorry."

Ben sits down. Ryan is beaming at him and the eye not hidden by the patch is dancing. Ben puts the invitation in his desk and goes back to drawing the golden toad. Before he knows it, Ryan is peering over his shoulder.

"Cool. What's that?"

"A toad," Ben says. He keeps it short, hoping Ryan will leave him alone.

"Cool. It's yellow!"

"It's called a golden toad."

"Can I see?"

Ben stares at Ryan, but being stared at doesn't bother him.

"Please?" Ryan says.

Ben holds the book up. Ryan grabs for it, but drops it.

"Ryan!" Ben says. The kid can be such a jerk!

Ryan scrambles to pick it up, then starts flipping through the pages. "Cool! This is the coolest book! Cool!"

"Ryan!" Mrs. Kutcher's voice is sharp. "Are you doing your work?"

"No! I'm looking at Ben's book. It's really cool!"

"Both of you come up here, please," she says.

Ben gives Ryan a murderous look, but Ryan doesn't notice. He's already halfway to Mrs. Kutcher's desk.

"You two both need to get to work. Neither of you can afford just sitting around while everybody else does what needs doing."

"But I was trying to work!" Ben says. "He was the one that was talking."

"I just wanted to see the book," Ryan says.

"All right, all right. Whatever happened, put the book away. You're supposed to be doing spelling."

Ben starts to protest, but Mrs. Kutcher shakes her head, stopping him. "Please don't argue. Just do your work."

Ben goes back to his chair and sits there with his arms folded.

He can hear Ryan trying to get his attention.

Frankie Mirley snickers.

Ben doesn't look up.

Right after he gets home from school the next day, Ben tosses his backpack onto the sofa and hurries into his backyard. He hikes down the trail, going past the marshy place where he caught the peeper. The sun is shining, and he goes deeper and deeper into the woods—farther than he's ever gone before. He's a little nervous about finding his way back, but it seems like someone has made a trail there; it's faint but he can follow it all right. Ben likes being alone. He'll turn back before he gets lost.

The trail makes a sharp bend to the right and Ben stops. It feels like he's been here before. About twenty yards ahead is another trail that leads past some rock outcrops and heads up a small hill. He takes a few steps and looks around.

This is the path he and Mrs. Tibbets explored last Saturday! His family's land not only backs up to Mrs. Tibbets's property, the two places are connected by a system of trails. He hurries up the path and comes to the vernal pool. He sits on the big rock beside it for a moment, but he's too excited about his discovery to sit still. He jumps up and takes the path toward Mrs. Tibbets's house. Maybe he'll just knock on the door and say hi. The trail leads him to her backyard—the garage is right in front of him.

Ben walks around to the driveway, but Mrs. Tibbets's car

isn't there. He looks in the kitchen window. He can see dishes in the sink and jars and plates spread out on the counter, but no sign of her. When Ben turns away from the door, he sees a car pull in the driveway. It looks familiar. The door swings open, and as soon as he sees the red hair, he knows who it is: Mrs. Tibbets's sister-in-law. Ben can't escape. He just stands there on the walk as the woman heads towards him.

"Oh!" she says when he sees him.

"Hi," Ben says.

"Who are you?"

"I'm Ben Moroney," Ben says. "I'm one of Mrs. Tibbets's students."

The woman frowns. Ben looks at her and then, instinctively, thrusts his hand out. She looks at it like she doesn't want to take it, but then she does. Her hand is dry and bony.

"I'm Mrs. Tibbets's sister-in-law," she says, "Tabitha Turner. Where is she?"

Ben shakes his head. "No one's home. I just came over to...I mean...sometimes I do work around the house for her."

Tabitha Turner exhales with disgust. "Of course she's not here! What was I thinking? Just because she said she'd be here means absolutely nothing." She glances at her watch. "I don't have time for this." She looks at Ben like she's not sure why he's still there.

"Um...I'll probably just go ahead and leave now."

“Well, I can’t wait around here any longer,” Mrs. Turner says, heading back to her car.

“The woods here are really nice,” Ben says. “It’s a nice place.” The words are out of his mouth before he realizes what he’s saying.

Tabitha Turner stops in the driveway and turns slowly. “Has she been talking to you about this land? What did she say to you?”

“Nothing. She just took me on a walk through the woods and showed me all the things that are living around here.”

Tabitha Turner shakes her head again and blows air out through her mouth in a violent burst. “Oh. That woman.”

She gets in her car and Ben watches her pull out of the driveway. He goes back to the kitchen door and looks inside one more time. As he heads toward the woods, he spots the cage under the lean-to by the garage. He stops, then takes a few steps closer. There’s no movement inside the cage. He approaches it and puts his face close to the wire. It’s too dark in the little enclosure to see anything.

Ben whistles, thinking he might wake whatever it is.

“Hey!” he says, and gives the cage a gentle shake. He still doesn’t see anything, but he thinks he hears something move inside the closed-off part of the cage.

Now he’s really curious. *I won’t bother them,* he thinks. *I just want to get a look at what kind of snakes live in the cage.*

Ben looks around. Thick grass grows in tall clumps, but he sees a stick about two feet long lying by the side of the garage. He picks it up and very carefully pushes it through the crack along the edge of the door. He manages to maneuver the stick into the small entrance to the enclosure, but he can't get it in far enough. There's too much of an angle.

Now figuring this out has become a challenge. Ben forgets about Mrs. Tibbets's warning. He gives the cage another shake, but nothing happens.

The cage door is held closed with a hasp. A twist tie, something you'd use on plastic bags, holds the hasp closed. *If I open the door a tiny bit,* Ben thinks, *I can get the stick into the nesting area and move it around a little. Then I'll close the door quickly as soon as the snake shows itself.*

Ben carefully unwinds the tie on the hasp and takes it off, stuffing it in his jacket pocket. He tries to pull back on the door, but the cage is old and the door sticks a little. He gives it a harder yank, and it pops open. There's still no movement from the closed-off area, so he slides the stick in along the floor, keeping the door open just enough for the width of the stick. He pushes it into the enclosure and moves it around.

There's something in there. He tries to slide the stick underneath it and lift it a little—he doesn't want to poke it. Whatever it is, it's heavy, and it moves against the stick.

Then he sees it.

A dark triangular head emerges from the hole in the closed-off area. Ben's heart starts thumping. It's definitely a poisonous snake, but he's not sure what kind. Its tongue flicks out, testing the air in the cage. The snake freezes at the entrance of the hidden part of the cage.

Just as Ben is thinking he should close the cage door, he hears a car pull in the driveway. *Mrs. Tibbets is back.* He doesn't think it's possible for his heart to beat any faster, but it does. He pulls the stick out of the cage and slams the cage door, but it bounces back open—it's a little warped and doesn't fit very well.

Now the snake is slowly pulling itself out of the enclosure. Ben's mind races in a million different directions at once. With one hand he digs in his pocket, feeling for the little tie that sealed the door, and with the other hand he tries to force the cage shut. He hears the car door open and close. Ben knows that Mrs. Tibbets will come up the walkway between the garage and the house and that she'll be able to see him from there if she bothers to look over. He gives up searching for the twist tie and presses both hands flat against the wire of the door, trying to close it all the way.

The snake glides around the side of the cage. Its skin is a mottled tan with dark brown stripes, its underside a yellowish white. The tail part is dark with a rattle on the end.

Ben breathes more quickly as he sees the size of this creature—three or four feet long and as thick around as his forearm. He imagines it striking out and biting his hand. His heart pounds. Then he sees another triangular head emerge from the nesting area. There are two of them.

"Hello? Is someone there?"

He can't see Mrs. Tibbets, but she must have heard him.

Ben's back is prickly with sweat and fear. He shoves the door as tight as it will go. His only hope is to distract Mrs. Tibbets and pretend that he's just gotten here, then come back in a minute and make sure the snake hasn't gotten out. With one last push on the door, Ben steps away from the cage and walks out in a wide circle, away from the garage, as if he's just come from the woods. He still can't see her.

"Hello?" he calls out. "Is that you, Mrs. Tibbets?" He heads quickly toward the walkway, keeping a distance from the back of the garage where the cage is.

"Oh, Ben! What a surprise!" Mrs. Tibbets is smiling. Ben waves and takes a quick glance at the cage. The door has swung wide open. But it's too late to do anything about that, at least right now.

"Hi!" he says, hoping his voice doesn't sound too quivery. "I was walking out in back of my house. I found this trail, and then I recognized where I was."

"Oh, how wonderful!" Mrs. Tibbets said. She's holding two big bags of groceries. "I thought there was a way through there, but it's been a long time since I've explored that part of the woods. Here, hold these, please, while I unlock my back door."

She hands Ben the bags of groceries while she fumbles with her keys. The cage is just out of view. Ben feels like he wants to throw up, but he has to stand there calmly, pretending that nothing's wrong.

"Why don't you come in for just a minute?" she asks as she opens the door. "You can put the groceries over there."

There's nothing Ben can do but walk in and put the bags on the counter. "I ought to get back," he says, desperate to escape.

"Don't be silly. You came all this way. Stay for a minute. Let me see what I have here for a quick snack."

"That would be great, Mrs. Tibbets, but I really have to go. My mom doesn't know where I am or anything."

"Well, all right," she says, and Ben makes a beeline for the door. "Oh, wait!" she says. "I forgot. I've got something for you."

Ben follows her out the door along the walkway. Terrified that she's going to walk toward the lean-to, he tries to think of something to do, some way to stop her. But she goes right to the garage, opens the door, and disappears in the dark coolness.

Ben sticks his head in. The garage is piled high with things. You couldn't park a car in it if you had to.

"I saw it the other day and meant to give it to you," Mrs. Tibbets says as she squeezes between a pile of tools and a stack of boxes. "Oh, here it is."

She holds up a short-handled net. "This should help you with those peepers."

"Thanks," Ben says. Half an hour ago, he would have been thrilled and eager to tell her he had caught a peeper with his bare hands. Now he just wants to get away from here. "That's great. I really have to go."

"All right," she says. "I'll see you at school tomorrow. And remember, the night of the spadefoots could happen any day now. I hope you'd still like to come."

"Yeah, sure," Ben says. He walks out of the garage with Mrs. Tibbets a few feet behind him. Instead of heading directly for the woods, Ben hangs back, praying that Mrs. Tibbets won't decide to go check out the cage. "Thanks a lot!" he says.

Mrs. Tibbets stands at her back door for a moment waving at him, then steps inside and shuts it.

Ben walks around to the side of the garage and stops. He waits for a minute, then tiptoes back to the lean-to. The door to the cage is wide open. He sucks in a deep breath and walks over for a closer look. The snakes aren't in the outer area of the cage. He lets out his breath all at once, like he's been holding it for an hour. He glances around his feet for any glimpse of them, but tells himself they probably just slithered back into their nest. He fumbles in his pocket for the twist tie, shuts the door as tight as he can get it, and then flaps down the hasp. His fingers are shaking. It's a struggle, but he finally manages to fasten it with the tie.

Ben knows he should have checked to make sure the snakes were definitely in there, but he tears across the field and plunges into the woods. Frantic to get home, he barely even glances at the vernal pool. As he approaches the path that leads to his backyard, he realizes that he's gripping the net Mrs. Tibbets gave him.

Chapter Nine

The next day in class Ben can barely look up at Mrs. Tibbets. He slumps down in his seat, thinking about the snakes. He knows that snakes don't ordinarily strike people—at least if people leave them alone—but he can't help picturing them gliding out of the cage, lurking in the garden, ready to strike out if someone passes by. Someone like Mrs. Tibbets. He sits up straight and tries to concentrate on the class discussion, but he can't get those two triangular heads out of his mind.

When Ben gets home he has a snack, then goes to his room and shuts the door. He doesn't know what else to do but work on his homework. He stares at his geography assignment. An outline of the report is due tomorrow, but Ben hasn't been able to get started on it. Now it's the last thing he wants to do. The desert seems a million miles away.

The phone rings. Ben runs into the hall and answers it.

"Ben? This is Mrs. Tibbets."

Ben is too stunned to speak. He stares at the wall.

"Ben?"

"Oh, right. Hi."

"I need to ask you something."

"Okay." Ben's heart is racing.

"When you came by yesterday afternoon, did you notice anything about the cage behind my garage?"

"What?" Ben is fighting for time.

"The cage behind my garage—the one under the lean-to."

Now Ben's mind is racing, too. He knows he should confess, but he just can't.

"Um...no. I didn't notice anything."

"Well, someone apparently opened the cage and then fastened it shut again." She stops talking for a moment, leaving space for him to say something if he wants to. "Ben, the snakes in that cage are dangerous. Somehow they got out."

"Wow." Ben's voice is barely above a whisper. He feels terrible about the lie. But he can't bring himself to explain everything to her. "What kind of snakes were they?" he asks.

"Rattlesnakes. Timber rattlers. That's why I asked you to stay away from them."

"Rattlesnakes?" Ben tries to sound surprised.

"Yes. I thought maybe you were looking at them when you were here."

"Um, no," says Ben.

"Oh, this is horrible. I shouldn't have kept them."

"Where did you get them?" Ben tries to sound like he's just interested and doesn't know anything about them.

"They're very rare around here," Mrs. Tibbets says. "My husband was licensed to capture and move snakes that had lost their habitat. He was going to transfer those rattlers, and then he...." She pauses for a minute, and Ben knows she's thinking about her husband dying.

She takes a breath and goes on. "I should have done something with them. Now, who knows what happened? Maybe there was a hole in the cage. They got out somehow."

"Maybe someone stole them," Ben says.

"It's hard to imagine. No one knew they were there. Oh, what have I done?"

"You...you didn't do anything," Ben says.

"Yes, I did. I kept them and I shouldn't have."

"Will they be all right?"

"I don't know." The teacher's voice sounds so sad that Ben's throat tightens. "It's too early in the year for them to be out, and they usually can't adapt to a new habitat. This is all my fault."

"Maybe they'll be okay," Ben says, trying to cheer her up. And himself.

"Thanks." Then, before Ben can hang up, she asks, "Is your mother there?"

Ben freezes. *Why does she want my mom?* "Um...yeah," he stammers.

"May I speak with her?"

Ben feels sick. "Sure. Just a minute."

He calls his mom.

"Who is it?" she asks.

"It's Mrs. Tibbets." He hands her the phone and walks away. But as soon as he's around the corner, he stops to listen. His mother says hello, and then falls silent. She's quiet for a long time. He sticks his head around the corner, and sees her just standing there with the phone to her ear.

"Are you sure?" she says. Then, after a pause, she talks for a while, saying how much Ben has always liked the outdoors and wild things, and how she appreciates Mrs. Tibbets's concern. She hangs up and sees Ben watching.

"I wish you'd told us about those snakes," she says.

Ben nods. If his mom asks him whether he let them out, he knows he'll have to tell her the truth. "Well," she says, "I'm relieved you didn't have anything to do with it. She sounded very upset."

His mom heads back to the kitchen. Ben stands there. He's missed his chance to let the truth come out. Sinking deeper and deeper into a hole, he feels worse than ever.

He goes back to his desk and stares at the blank wall. The desert is *two* million miles away now. When he closes his eyes, he sees the snakes. He wonders where they are tonight.

Ben does his best to avoid Mrs. Tibbets in school that week and the next. When he's in her class he does his work but doesn't raise his hand. Twice she asks him after class if he's managed to catch a peeper, or if he wants to come check on the vernal pool again. Both times he shakes his head and hurries out of the room.

It's not like he's lost interest in the toads, though. He spends a lot of time in the woods behind his house. His parents must notice, because one day his father comes home with a new pair of waders.

"This is to save your sneakers," he says.

They fit him better than the ones that he used at Mrs. Tibbets's house, and he likes the feeling of being waterproof. Using the net Mrs. Tibbets gave him, Ben snares a few American toads, but he still doesn't manage to catch another peeper. He decides to keep one of the toads, and with the money he's saved he buys a terrarium from the pet store. After fixing it up with some mud and a couple of plants, Ben settles the toad in its new habitat.

The following Thursday afternoon Ben is sitting at his desk at home, trying to get started on his geography project. His mom has laid down the law: no more wandering in the woods until he's made progress on his report. His sister is away playing with Rory, Ryan's sister. The house is quiet. He has no excuse for putting this off any longer. He stares at the report guidelines. He picks up a pencil and taps it on his notebook. He loves the desert. Why can't he get started on this report?

Frustrated, he looks around the room until his gaze comes to rest on a book about amphibians he brought home from the school library. He picks it up and starts leafing through it. He glances over at the terrarium. The toad is crouched in the corner. It doesn't look happy. Four glass walls and some dirt and plants don't make much of a home for something that's used to living outside in the wild. He skims through the section of the book on building a terrarium for amphibians, looking for ideas.

Just then the doorbell rings.

"I'll get it," he yells, slamming the book shut. He runs down the hallway to the front door, happy for an excuse to escape his homework. He opens the door and finds his sister Agatha standing there. Ryan is just behind her, holding a book in his hands.

"The door was locked, you bozo," Agatha says and shoves past him.

"It was not. Try turning the knob for once." Ben turns back to Ryan. "Hi," he says.

"Hi," Ryan says. "Mom and Rory are waiting in the car, so

I can't stay. I brought your book back. And when I was at the library I found these books about amphibians—and reptiles, too. I thought you might want to see them." He's so excited he practically throws the books at Ben and they fall to the floor between them. "Whoops!" he says and scrambles to pick them up. "I took them out on my library card and my mom said we could bring them over. You can give them back to me when you're done."

Ben helps Ryan with the books and Ryan just keeps on talking.

"They're not as cool as your book. Your book is the best. I've read some of the chapters twice already and—"

Ryan's mother honks the horn and waves for Ryan to hurry.

"Sorry, gotta go."

"Thanks," Ben says.

Ryan smiles his loopy smile. "See you tomorrow," he says. On his way to the car he turns back and calls out, "Oh, yeah. I put a picture I drew in one of the books. It's for you."

"Okay," Ben says. He waves good-bye as Ryan's mom backs the car out of the driveway. Ben looks down at the stack of books in his arms. Still standing in the doorway with the door open, he opens up the top book. Between the first two pages is a colored-pencil drawing. It's beautiful—much better than anything Ben's ever done. He didn't even know Ryan could draw.

It's a picture of a bright orange creature perched on a rock by a stream. Above it, Ryan has written in large block letters:

GOLDEN TOAD—ENDANGERED OR EXTINCT

HANDLE WITH CARE!

Underneath the picture of the toad Ryan has written an inscription:

For Ben. Your friend, Ryan.

Ben's embarrassed. He hasn't done anything to deserve Ryan's friendship. He's barely even talked to him.

He takes the books to his room. He searches through his desk drawer for the tape dispenser and sticks Ryan's picture on the wall above his desk.

Then he sits at the desk and looks at the library books Ryan brought. He opens the biggest book first, the one with the glossy color photograph of a bright red frog on the cover. He thumbs through, looking at all the different species of frogs and toads, then he stops on a page and stares at the photograph of a small, smooth-skinned, olive green toad. Two yellow stripes curve across its back. Its eyes are bright. The edges of the eyes are golden, and the pupils are vertical—up and down—not horizontal like other toads'. A diagram shows the projections on the hind feet; they look like little shovels. He reads the caption:

Eastern spadefoot, now rare and endangered in several states.

It's the toad Mrs. Tibbets told him about, the kind that appears every year in her vernal pool!

Compared to some of the other species in this book, it doesn't look like much. But Mrs. Tibbets had made it sound like a treasure, like a special secret that only the two of them know about. An endangered species right around the corner from where he lives.

Ben thinks about the toads out there buried way under the ground, waiting for the rain. He'd love to see them when they come out for that one night. But that would mean talking to Mrs. Tibbets, and that's something he can't imagine doing, not after what happened with the snakes. His guilt sits in the pit of his stomach like a big cold stone. He reads all there is about the spadefoot, and it only makes him feel worse.

"Ben," his mother calls. "It's time for dinner."

He looks at the spadefoot one more time and closes the book. He'll have to work on his report later.

Chapter Ten

When Ben walks into science class the next day, four or five kids are crowded around Mrs. Tibbets's desk. He edges closer to see what they're gaping at: a large glass jar with three frogs partially hidden in the mud and grass at the bottom.

"Peepers," he says.

"Nuh-uh," Frankie says, grabbing for the jar. "It's frogs. Here, I'll shake 'em up so you can see 'em better."

Ben starts to grab for the jar before the frogs get hurt. Just then, Mrs. Tibbets walks into the room and everybody takes a step back except for Frankie, who's got the jar in his hands.

"Put it down, Frankie," Mrs. Tibbets says calmly. Frankie rolls his eyes and puts the jar back on the desk.

"Everybody in your seats," the teacher says. "You'll all have a chance to take a look at our friends here."

The students straggle back to their desks. When the room is quiet, Mrs. Tibbets holds up the jar and turns it around slowly. "These little guys are hard to find, but now is a good time to catch them."

"You caught them yourself?" Frankie asks.

"Of course."

"Cool," says Ryan. "Can I see one?"

"You can see them from there. I'm not letting them out today."

There are pleads and groans, but Mrs. Tibbets ignores them. "Has anyone ever seen one outside?"

Several kids shake their heads.

"You may not have seen them, but I'll bet some of you have heard them," Mrs. Tibbets says. She looks at Ben. "How about you, Ben?"

"Yeah," he says, not looking her in the eye. "They're spring peepers. I've heard them behind my house."

"Can you make their sound for us?" Mrs. Tibbets asks.

Ben hesitates.

"Come on, Ben," Ryan says.

Ben can feel everyone looking at him. He shrugs. "I don't know. It's sort of a high peeping sound." He tries to imitate a peeper: *"Eeep...eeep...eeep..."*

A couple of kids laugh, but Jenny says, "Oooooh, I've heard that noise. I heard it every night last week."

"Me, too," someone else chimes in.

"Let's try it," says Mrs. Tibbets. "Let's make a peeper chorus."

All the kids start making peeping noises. They're having a great time. Making noise in class is something no one ever lets them do. Mrs. Tibbets gives them about thirty seconds, then signals for quiet.

"Those little frogs make that big a noise?" Frankie asks.

"They sure do," Mrs. Tibbets says, almost laughing. "Other amphibians make even louder noises. You can hear a bunch of spadefoots from a long, long way away when they're singing."

"What are spadefoots?" Ryan asks.

"I'm talking about spadefoot toads," Mrs. Tibbets explains. "Their name comes from the rough, shovel-like growths on their back feet. They use them like little spades to burrow into the ground."

"What do they sound like?" Jenny asks.

"Like a big flock of crows cawing," the teacher says, "or some say they sound like hundreds of balloons being rubbed together."

"I haven't heard a noise like that," Jenny says.

"Well, spadefoot toads are very rare around here. In fact, they're listed as a threatened species in our state. And they only come out one or two nights a year, usually after a rainy spell in April." Mrs. Tibbets smiles. "If we get a good rain next week, there's a good chance they'll be out."

"Why only one night?" Ryan blurts out.

"They don't have much time," the teacher says, "because they only lay their eggs in pools that dry up."

"Vernal pools," says Ben.

Mrs. Tibbets gives him a nod. "Right, Ben. They choose temporary pools because their eggs will be safer there. There are no fish to gobble them up. But since these pools don't last long, they all have to work fast together. The males come out and sing, then the females come out and lay their eggs. The males fertilize the eggs. In two days the tadpoles hatch, and within a month they hop away as toadlets. So it's all over very quickly. Most people don't even know they're there."

"What happens to them then?" asks Jenny.

"They dig deep holes in the ground with their back feet and bury themselves in the wet earth. Up to eight feet deep! They stay there most of the time. That's why you can't find them during the rest of the year."

"It would be cool to see them," Ryan says.

"Well, I was thinking..." Mrs. Tibbets lowers her voice almost to a whisper, like she's telling a ghost story. A sly smile spreads across her face. Everyone leans a little closer. "If some of you were interested, we might have a little field trip one night next week. It just so happens I have a pool on my land where the spadefoots come to breed. Would you like that?"

The kids all yell their approval.

"How many of you think you might come?"

Half the class raises their hands. Ben feels empty inside—like something that belonged to him is being given away to others who don't care nearly as much as he does. He's dying to go, but he doesn't raise his hand.

"I've made some permission slips, and people who are interested need to take one and bring it back signed. Your parents will have to bring you to my house and pick you up afterwards. I'll have to let you know at the last minute what day it will be, though. We'll just have to watch the weather."

"What day do you *think* it will be?" Ryan asks.

"Well, they're forecasting rain for Wednesday or Thursday. Let's hope they're right. I don't think your parents will want you going on a field trip on the weekend."

When Mrs. Tibbets hands out the permission slips, Ben takes one and stuffs it into his backpack.

On the way back to Mrs. Kutcher's class, Frankie sneers, "Who wants to go in the woods with the Frog Lady? *Urrrrrp!* Not me."

I do, Ben thinks. *But I can't.*

"Wait," Frankie yells. "Her name isn't Mrs. Tibbets. It's Mrs. Ribbets! *Ribbet...ribbet.*" He guffaws. He's beside himself at how funny he is.

Ben just glares at him.

The next Monday half of the class brings in their permission slips. The other half either can't go or doesn't want to. Ben's permission slip is still in his backpack, unsigned.

There's no rain that day or the next day. It's like Massachusetts has changed almost overnight from a cold, dark, rainy, muddy place into a sunny world full of life. The skies are blue every day, and the temperature rises into the sixties. On Wednesday a few kids wear shorts to school.

"Is it going to be tonight?" Ryan asks Mrs. Tibbets. He's asked that same question at least two dozen times over the past two days.

"It doesn't look like it," the teacher says. "It's got to really rain hard."

Ben watches, feeling farther and farther away from everything and everybody.

"But what happens if it doesn't rain enough?" Janice asks.

"The spadefoots will wait until next year," Mrs. Tibbets says. "They can wait three or four years before they lay eggs."

"Four years! We'll *never* see them!" Ryan wails.

"Nature takes its time," Mrs. Tibbets says. "Unlike most people, nature is very patient."

Thursday starts out sunny. But by nine o'clock in the morning, in the middle of reading, the skies start to darken. By the time Ben gets to Mrs. Tibbets's class, it looks like it could start raining any second.

"Tonight?" Ryan asks. "Is it tonight?"

"I don't think so," Mrs. Tibbets says. "Most scientists think that the spadefoots get their message from the rain seeping into the soil, so the ground won't be soaked enough tonight."

"But what if it happens over the weekend?" someone asks. "We'll miss it."

"Let's just wait and see what happens," Mrs. Tibbets says.

The skies stay gray. The clouds thicken and the air feels damp and heavy. But the rain doesn't come.

At home that night Ben spreads out everything he has so far for his geography report. He's downloaded information off the Internet and made notes on some index cards. But he can't seem to get interested. It all seems dry and boring. He's staring at the wall above his desk when he hears the phone ring.

"Ben," his mother calls, "it's Toby!"

Finally! Ben thinks. He's been sending his friend e-mails for days and hasn't heard back. He even called a couple of times and left messages.

"Lizardman!" he says as he picks up the phone.

"Hi," Toby answers. His voice sounds uneasy.

"How's Arizona?"

"Okay. How's Massachusetts?"

"It stinks, as usual," Ben says.

"Too bad," says Toby.

Ben waits for Toby to say more, but he doesn't. He wonders why Toby called if he doesn't want to talk. Toby's always easy to talk to. The silence at the other end of the line feels strange. "How's Lenny?" Ben asks.

"Um, well...that's why I'm calling." Toby's voice is tight and thin. "My mom said I should."

Ben grips the receiver to his ear.

"Something happened," Toby finally goes on. "He got sick or something. And I found him in the terrarium."

"Wait," Ben says. "You mean he died? He's dead?"

"Yeah, I don't know. I didn't mean to..."

They're both silent for a moment.

"I'm really sorry, Ben."

"Didn't you feed him right?" Ben feels tears welling up in his eyes. "What were you feeding him?"

"No! I did! I mean... Dad said maybe he was old, or maybe he didn't like the change when he came to my house, or—"

"But you were supposed to take care of him!"

"I know! It wasn't my fault. I didn't..."

Ben can tell that Toby is close to tears, too. He doesn't know what to say. He's afraid he's going to get so mad he'll say something really stupid.

"Okay," Ben mutters. "I'll talk to you later."

"Okay, yeah. Okay. I'm sorry."

Ben hangs up first. He puts his jacket on and goes outside where no one can see or hear him. *This is stupid,* he tells himself. *The dumb lizard was two thousand miles away. You probably never would have seen him again anyway.* But Ben feels like he's lost more than a pet.

He sits down on the back steps and stares out at the woods behind his house. The spring peepers are calling and so are the American toads. He looks up—he can't see any stars. He wonders when the rain will start, and that makes him think of the spadefoots. He'd love to see them. But that would mean he'd have to talk to Mrs. Tibbets. Thinking about Mrs. Tibbets makes him think about the snakes and his dead lizard, and it just goes around and around in circles until his stomach tightens up again.

"Ben! Are you out there?" his father calls out the back door. The light comes on.

"Yeah," Ben answers.

"What are you doing?"

"Listening," he says.

"Well, it's time to come in. Unless you're planning on spending the night out there."

That sounds like a good idea to Ben. At least out here he wouldn't have to deal with people. But he gets up and trudges onto the back porch.

"You okay?" his father asks.

Ben nods. "Yeah. Just wondering if it's going to rain."

"Feels like it to me."

Ben tries to slip by his father, but his father grabs his shoulder and looks at him. "You sure you're okay?"

"My lizard died," Ben says. He knows it's more than that, but it's the simplest thing to say. His father wraps his arms around Ben and just holds him there for a while. Ben buries his face in his father's sweater. It smells like his dad.

"Things will look better in the morning," his dad says. "Why don't you give it up and go to bed?'

Ben nods. He goes back into his room and puts on his pajamas. He doesn't really care about his homework. He doesn't care much about anything.

Ben wakes up in the middle of the night. Sheets of rain are lashing against the windows of his room. He burrows down in the blankets. He's like a spadefoot deep down in the earth. He falls asleep listening to the sounds of the rainstorm.

It's still raining when Ben gets up. At breakfast he goes through his backpack, finds the permission slip from Mrs. Tibbets, and asks his mom to sign it. She reads it over and frowns.

"Ben, it says here that this is for a weeknight."

"But it didn't happen yet. And it might happen tonight, because it's raining now."

"But I can't imagine that she'll have kids come over to her house on a Friday night."

"But what if she does? Just sign it, please?" Ben pleads.

His mother signs the paper and hands it back to him. "You're lucky to have a teacher who will spend time with you outside of school," she says.

"Yeah," Ben says. "I know."

Ben doesn't have science on Fridays, but after lunch he goes to Mrs. Tibbets's room. She's sitting at her desk, peeling an orange.

"Hi, Mrs. Tibbets," he says.

"Hello, Ben."

He walks over and hands her the permission slip.

"This is a little late," she says. "I thought there was some reason you didn't want to come."

"I know." Ben takes a deep breath and clears his throat. "But I was thinking...um...if you're going to look at the spadefoots, I'd like to come."

Mrs. Tibbets puts down her orange and peers at Ben.

"There's no field trip now," she says. "I said I'd only do it on a weeknight. It's Friday."

"I know, but..." Ben can feel the secret inside him trying to work its way out. But he can't tell her what happened—he just can't. He swallows. "But I still want to come with you to look for the spadefoots."

"Have your parents call me," Mrs. Tibbets says. "If it's okay with them, then I'd love to have you."

"Okay," says Ben. "Do you think tonight's the night?"

"Seems like it to me. It's now or never."

"Okay," says Ben. "I'll bring my new boots."

"New boots, huh?" says Mrs. Tibbets with a smile. "Okay. I'll be waiting to hear from your parents."

"Are you almost ready?" Ben's mom calls out. "Mrs. Tibbets said she'll be by for you in ten minutes."

"I'm ready now," Ben says, hurrying into the living room.

"I want to go, too," whines Agatha.

"You don't even like frogs!" Ben wonders if there is actually a chance his parents would let her go. He hopes not.

"I told you no, Aggie," Mrs. Moroney says. "You have a gymnastics meet tomorrow. You'll need to be in bed early."

"I still want to go," Agatha says.

"You still can't," Ben says.

“Humph,” Agatha says. She spins on her heels and heads off to her room.

Ben parks himself on the arm of the sofa where he can see the street. It seems like he’s waiting forever, but finally Mrs. Tibbets’s old station wagon pulls into his driveway.

“Are you sure you want to go out tonight?” his mom asks. “It’s really pouring.”

Ben rolls his eyes. “It has to be raining, Mom. That’s when they show up.”

“You’re going to get soaked,” his mother says, smiling. He can tell that she’s happy he’s going.

“I’ve got a raincoat,” Ben says. “And these.” He holds up his new boots.

His mother shakes her head. “Well, you wouldn’t catch me wading around in all that muck.” She reaches to zip up his coat. She can’t help herself.

“Mom, I can do it,” he says.

He pulls his hood over his head and dashes out the door.

“You ready?” Mrs. Tibbets asks once he hops in the car. Ben nods. “Good. You can put the waders on when we get back to the house,” she says. “You’re going to need them.”

They drive through the night with the rain pattering on the car roof and the tires hissing over the wet roads. Mrs.

Tibbets keeps a one-way conversation going the whole time. He hasn't seen anyone this excited since they took his sister Agatha to ride horses on her seventh birthday.

"I've never seen a more perfect night. I just can't wait. I'm wondering how many there'll be this year. The last time I was out on the right night, there must've been a dozen pairs. We'll just have to see."

"A dozen pairs? That's all?" Ben asks. That doesn't seem like very many to him.

"That's all. Of course, when my husband and I first started counting them, there were lots more. And as far as I know, no one else has ever spotted any spadefoots in the area. We found a few other vernal pools, but no spadefoots. Ours is the only place—"

Mrs. Tibbets cuts her sentence short and Ben looks over at her.

"There must be some other ones around somewhere," he says.

"I don't know. There aren't many left. The state now lists them as threatened, on the verge of being endangered."

"You mean *endangered,* like almost extinct? Like the golden toads down in Costa Rica?"

"Right. There are still plenty of eastern spadefoots in other states, but their numbers have really dwindled in Massachusetts."

"Why?"

"Well, it's the farthest north they live. There are fewer and fewer places for them to call home. Too many people. Too many trees coming down and houses going up. Habitat loss..." She flips on her turn signal and slows down. "But let's not talk about that. Tonight our mission is to see how they're doing."

Mrs. Tibbets leans over the steering wheel and peers through the windshield. She slows even more until they're barely moving.

"What are you doing?"

"Looking for toads. Or salamanders. This is the place where they hop over the road to get to the pool. I find a couple of squished toads every year. Look! There's something moving right there!"

Mrs. Tibbets steps on the brakes and they lurch to a stop in the middle of the road.

She's crazy! Ben thinks, but then he sees a small form in the beam of the headlights.

"Go look, Ben. See what it is!"

Ben looks both ways for cars—the road is quiet and dark in either direction—then he opens his door.

"Be careful," Mrs. Tibbets warns.

He trots out in front of the station wagon, into the path of the headlights. There, fifteen feet from the car, is the small, huddled form of a toad. When Ben picks it up, it moves its hind legs feebly as if it's trying to get away, then hunches down in his hands.

Ben runs back to Mrs. Tibbets's side of the car, where she's rolled down the window. He holds out the toad, and Mrs. Tibbets shines the flashlight on it.

"Oh," she mutters. "It's just a regular old American toad. Dime a dozen. Still, it's cute." She strokes its head. Ben remembers how she kissed the frog in class. All right," she tells Ben, "take this little girl and put her on the other side of the road so she doesn't have to hop across it. She's so cold she's not moving very fast."

Ben carefully puts the toad in the wet grass on the side of the road and climbs back in the car. When Mrs. Tibbets pulls into her driveway and shuts off the engine, the rain sounds even louder on the roof of the car.

"You know, Ben, we make a good pair, you and me. Out hunting toads." She pockets her keys and opens the car door. "Everyone looking for a home."

Ben isn't sure what she means by that last remark, but she's out of the car before he can say anything. "Put the boots on," she calls to him. "Let's go in the backyard."

Ben pulls off his sneakers and opens the door so he can pull the big boots on. As soon as he climbs out of the car, Mrs. Tibbets is already scurrying around the side of the house, like a kid hurrying to see what's under the Christmas tree. He follows, the rain pattering on the hood of his jacket. He pulls it off his head and feels the cool wetness on his forehead and neck. As he comes around the side of the garage, he's nearly blinded by a bright light.

"Oh, sorry," says Mrs. Tibbets. The beam switches off, and he can see that she has strapped a light on her forehead so it moves wherever she turns her head.

"Come on!" She motions for him to follow and walks across the grass. When she reaches the edge of the woods, she stops so quickly that Ben bumps into her. She holds up her hand. "Shhhh," she says. "Just listen!"

Ben doesn't hear anything at first, at least not anything he hasn't heard already—the rain, the thunder off in the distance, the wind in the trees, the peepers calling, and the toads trilling.

"What?" he asks.

"Listen! There they are!"

Ben listens hard. Then he hears a layer of noise in a lower register. *Huuuuuh. Huuuuuh. Huuuuuh.* Like a tree full of crows cawing or a bunch of people snoring.

"Is that the spadefoots?" he asks. "That honking sound?"

"That's them."

They stand there a little while longer, just listening. Finally, without a word, Mrs. Tibbets gestures toward the woods.

Flashlights still off, they walk across the yard and across the field. The thunder crashes, closer now, and a torrent of rain sweeps past them, gusts of wind blowing the spidery branches of trees back and forth. Ben shivers. He has to hustle to stay close behind Mrs. Tibbets. This time she doesn't stop to look at tree bark or wildflowers. She doesn't even look back to make sure he's there. As they make their way through the woods, the calls get louder: spadefoot toad voices calling out one after another, grunting for all they're worth. Ben can't help but feel he's in a fairy tale, following a weird old magical woman deeper into a dark forest. He can't believe it's real.

Mrs. Tibbets stops at the edge of the pool. Dripping tree branches droop over the dark water. The pond looks bigger than it did the other day.

Mrs. Tibbets puts a finger against her lips. They stand and listen. A riot of sound rises and falls all around them. They're surrounded by a crazy orchestra—the wind in the trees, the thunder in the sky, the rain pattering on the pool and their jackets, the spring peepers chirping in the distance. And the little spadefoot toads right before them, leading the symphony.

Mrs. Tibbets steps into the pool and motions for Ben to follow. The moment she wades in, the spadefoot calls stop.

"It's all right," Mrs. Tibbets whispers. "They'll start again."

Even in wading boots Ben can feel the cold water around his feet and ankles and legs. He shivers again—he's not sure if it's from cold or excitement. They stand, silently waiting.

Huuuuuh. Huuuuuh.

Another starts up, then several more.

Huuuuuh.

Huuuuuh. Huuuuuh. Huuuuuh.

After a minute has passed, Ben figures there must be at least a dozen calling from different parts of the pool.

"There's a lot!" Mrs. Tibbets says. Even in the dark, Ben can see she's smiling, and he smiles back.

Then she laughs out loud, a high-pitched, girl-like giggle.

"Why are you laughing?"

"Oh, it's so silly!" she says.

"What?"

"My husband Thomas used to tell a story that he made up when he was little. He said that if you listen carefully when all the toads are out, you can hear the Overtoad."

"The Overtoad?"

"Right. It's something he made up—like the king of the toads, or the spirit toad that watches over all the toads and the places where they live. And when they're all calling out, the Overtoad joins in. We used to laugh about it. 'Watch out!' he'd say. 'It's a night for the Overtoad!'" Mrs. Tibbets makes a croaking sound. "Can you hear it, Ben? I think tonight is a night for the Overtoad!"

Ben loves the idea of the Overtoad. He almost expects to see it rise up over the pool, twenty-five feet tall, protecting all the little toads. He can't explain why, but he feels a chuckle welling up inside him. The laughter bubbles out of his throat and sets Mrs. Tibbets to laughing again. Ben tries to stifle his giggles, but the more she laughs, the more he does. This time, noise doesn't seem to bother the toads—they keep calling out.

Ben catches his breath, then tries to imitate the spadefoot sound. *Huuuuuh...huuuuuh.* Pretty close. Mrs. Tibbets makes a higher-pitched cawing noise. Both of them stand in the pool in the rain, adding their voices to the spadefoot chorus, calling out to the Overtoad. It's crazy and silly and amazing.

They're all saying, "We're here! We're here! We're alive! We're alive!"

Mrs. Tibbets motions for Ben to come closer to her, and she switches on the light strapped around her head. She shines it around the pool, turning this way and that, then stops the beam on a branch sticking up out of the pool. She leans over so Ben can hear her above all the noise. "Look. There."

Ben sees the little spadefoot in the spotlight, resting on a branch floating on the surface of the water. Mrs. Tibbets wades over to it and Ben follows. She picks up the toad carefully and directs the light back to the branch. Just below it there's another toad swimming through the water. She scoops that one up, too, so she has one in each hand.

"This is the male—the one that was calling. Here's the female." She turns it over. "See how fat it is? It has a bunch of eggs to lay. Here. Take a toad."

The male spadefoot crouches low in Ben's hand. It's smooth, not like the other toads he's held. He can clearly see the two yellow stripes on its back. The eyes are shiny metallic gold.

Mrs. Tibbets strokes her toad's head. "Just think," she says. "They come here every spring. This little pool has been the home for the ancestors of these toads for hundreds, maybe even thousands of years. They were probably here before people ever lived in this area."

"Wow," says Ben.

"Wow," Mrs. Tibbets repeats. "Cute little guy."

"Yeah." Ben can feel the toad's smooth belly on his palm. "Imagine a family living in a place for thousands of years."

"Imagine," says Mrs. Tibbets.

They let the toads slip back into the water and watch them swim to the branch.

"Let's count the couples," Mrs. Tibbets suggests.

Trying as best they can to avoid counting any toads twice, they wade around the pool looking and listening for the spadefoots. Working in the rain for half an hour, they come up with sixteen pairs and six individuals.

"That's several more than last year!" Mrs. Tibbets says.

"Great!"

"It is great. It's wonderful. I think we're all done."

They wade out of the pool and stand on its edge, very close to one another. It's still noisy, with the rain and wind and thunder and toads and frogs, but Ben feels quiet inside. And suddenly, clearly, he knows it's time.

"Mrs. Tibbets...?"

"Yes, Ben?"

"I let your snakes go."

She turns her head. She's still got her headlamp on, and the bright light hurts his eyes. He can barely make out the details of her mouth and eyes and nose. She's looking right at him. He holds his breath, wondering what she'll say.

"Oh," she says.

Ben shuts his eyes to keep out the light. "It was an accident. I didn't mean to. I was curious, but I shouldn't have messed with the cage. I'm really sorry. I'm sorry if they got out and...died. I didn't mean for it to happen."

She doesn't speak. And then he feels her hand on his shoulder.

"It's all right, Ben," she says. "I'm sorry, too. But thank you for telling me."

The relief is tremendous. He doesn't know why, but he begins to cry. Great sobs come up from deep inside of him, catching him totally off guard. Mrs. Tibbets switches off her headlight and puts an arm around him. They stand there awkwardly by the side of the pool. The rain splats against their raincoats. Ben's body heaves up and down and he can't make it stop.

"I'm sorry." Ben takes a deep breath and lets his sobs subside. "I'm sorry," he repeats over and over. "I'm sorry."

"Or course you are," his teacher says over the sound of the rain. "Anyway, it doesn't really matter about the snakes now."

She pauses and then she says, "Maybe they'll find a new home somewhere else."

Wiping his face, Ben looks up at her. At first he thinks it's the rain, but then he sees there are tears on her cheeks, too. "Why are you crying?"

"Oh, I'm sorry, too."

"For me?"

"Yes, for you. And for all this." She sweeps her arm in a semicircle, gesturing to everything around her.

"What do you mean?"

"Nothing," she says.

"No, really. What are you sorry about?"

She shakes her head again.

"Does it have anything to do with what your sister-in-law said the other day?"

She doesn't answer.

"What's happening? Is it something about your home?"

"In a way."

"Why? How?"

"It's very complicated, Ben."

"Tell me, please," Ben says. He really wants to know. For a moment—for just a second—he doesn't see Mrs. Tibbets as a teacher. It's like he's looking at her through a magical pair of binoculars that shows who someone really is, not how they fit in his own little model of the world.

Mrs. Tibbets sniffs and laughs again, wiping the rain and tears from her cheek with the back of her hand. "Well, fair is fair. You told me your secret. I'll tell you mine. But let's do it inside over something warm. I love these toads, but I am certainly not one of them."

She turns away from the pool and heads down the trail toward the house.

The whole way back, Ben listens to the toads calling out, "We're here! We're alive! We're here."

Chapter Eleven

Mrs. Tibbets pours hot chocolate into Ben's cup and sits down at the kitchen table across from him. Outside, the rain beats on the windows.

Ben shivers again. His jeans are still a little damp and he feels chilly. He looks around Mrs. Tibbets's kitchen. It's cozy and cluttered. The boxes of pictures and papers are still sitting by the table.

Mrs. Tibbets sighs and leans forward, propping her elbows on the table. "Well, here's the problem," she says. "I only own the house and a little land around it. My sister-in-law owns the rest of the property, and she's going to sell it to a developer who plans to put up a bunch of houses."

"But I thought it was all yours," Ben says. "You live on it."

"No. My husband inherited the house and the yard, but his sister got everything else. He made her promise not to develop it right away after he died. But it's been over a year now, and she's got an eager buyer. She owns the land. She can do what she wants."

"But that's not fair," Ben says. "This is your home."

"Well, I could stay here and watch the bulldozers scrape away the trees and the workmen build the fancy houses, but I don't think I'd enjoy that very much. I'd rather go somewhere else."

"Couldn't you explain to your sister-in-law about the pond and the woods and—"

"She knows that. She grew up here."

"But why won't she listen to you?"

"The truth is, we don't get along very well, and never have. She's a practical woman who has little patience with what she calls my quirky ways. Thomas drove her crazy, too. Together, we just about made her pull her hair out. She's had her mind set on selling the property for years, but my husband kept talking her out of it. Also, I believe she thinks she's helping me. She sees me as an old woman whose house is a mess and who doesn't have any money, a woman about to lose her job."

"Lose your job? What do you mean?"

"Oh, Ben, I was away from teaching for a year after my husband died. When I decided to come back this winter, they had to find a spot for me somewhere. So they gave me a little place to teach science for the rest of the year. They didn't even really need a science teacher. Honestly, I don't think there's room for me there anymore. And I'm tired of jumping through their hoops."

Ben thinks about Mr. Nickelby and how he didn't seem to like her very much.

"Can they fire you?"

Mrs. Tibbets shakes her head. "They won't fire me. They'll just make it hard for me to stay. And maybe that's all right. I've taught a long, long time."

"But you're a great science teacher. They should be glad you came back." Ben's mind is reeling, trying to put all of the pieces of the puzzle together. "And you should still live on this land. It just doesn't seem fair."

"It's worse for the toads than for me," she says. "They don't have anywhere else to go."

Ben wishes he could think of a way to help her. He remembers books he's read and movies he's seen where the kids band together to help save a plot of land from the evil developers. He frowns. Those were just feel-good stories, nothing but make-believe. This is a lot more complicated. Still, there must be something he can do.

"Didn't you say spadefoots are listed as endangered in Massachusetts?" he asks.

"Yes, they're threatened, but—"

"Isn't it illegal to build houses where there are endangered animals? Can't you call someone and tell them about the toads? Someone from the government or something?"

Mrs. Tibbets sighs and she suddenly looks very old. "To save the toads, you have to save the habitat it lives in—have it certified as endangered. But it's hard to do. And if I did that, if I called someone, whatever's left of my relationship with Tabitha would fall apart. She'd never speak to me again. She's already found someone to build houses. Stopping it now would be like starting a war. "

Mrs. Tibbets looks out the window into the dark night. "I just don't have the stomach for it."

Ben looks at her. "Can't they just build houses somewhere else, away from the toads?"

"It's not that easy. The pool is close to the place where they'll need to build the road."

"They'll dig up the pool, or pave over it? But the toads are under there! Where will they go next spring?"

Mrs. Tibbets shakes her head, but she doesn't say anything.

"It's not fair," Ben says again. "It's not fair."

"Well, you know what they say," Mrs. Tibbets says. "Life's not fair."

"I hate it when people say that."

They sit there in silence. Ben wants to say something more, but he's run out of ideas. He had thought his own problems were confusing, but they're nothing compared to the problems in Mrs. Tibbets's life.

“I think I’ve said a little too much.” Mrs. Tibbets gets up and puts her raincoat back on. “I can see I’ve overwhelmed you, and I didn’t mean to do that. It’s time to get you home. Your parents will worry that you’re getting webbed feet in this weather.”

When Mrs. Tibbets stops her station wagon in Ben’s driveway, he climbs out.

“Thanks, Mrs. Tibbets,” he says.

“Thank you for coming. I was glad to have someone to share this incredible night with.”

Ben waves and closes the door. Halfway up the driveway, he turns back. Mrs. Tibbets rolls down her window.

“Yes?” she says.

“It’s still not fair.”

“Right,” says Mrs. Tibbets. “It’s not fair.”

“Maybe the Overtoad will eat all of them up!”

Chapter Twelve

After school on Monday, Ben sits at home in front of the computer. The notes for his geography report are scattered all over the desk—printouts about the Sonoran Desert, pictures of saguaro cactuses with mountains in the distance, maps of southern Arizona. So why can't he start writing his report?

Thinking about the desert makes him think about lizards.

Thinking about lizards makes him think about Lenny.

Thinking about Lenny makes him think about Toby.

He rummages through the pictures of the desert and stops at one he had almost forgotten. The heading says "Couch's spadefoot." It looks a lot like Mrs. Tibbets's spadefoots, except it has yellowish spots all over its back instead of the two stripes. *Weird that there are spadefoots in the desert, too,* he thinks. He reads the text under the drawing. There's no mention of it being endangered or threatened. *I guess the spadefoots haven't lost as much habitat down there,* Ben says to himself.

He wonders why Mrs. Tibbets isn't making more of an effort to stop the land from being sold. *The adult world is like a big wall,* Ben thinks. *You can't see through it, you can't get over it. How is a kid supposed to understand what they're doing on the other side?*

He types "Massachusetts spadefoots vernal pools" into the computer and looks at the search page. More than 800 listings come up. Some of them look pretty technical, but he clicks on about a dozen of them. Every time he sees the word "spadefoot" his heart leaps. This is his word. These are his spadefoots. He finds a page for kids that teaches about spadefoots and salamanders and vernal pools. He prints out a color photograph of an eastern spadefoot. But none of this is what he is looking for.

Then he comes across a reference to the Massachussetts Fisheries and Wildlife Natural Heritage and Endangered Species Program. It's an article about saving vernal pools. He tries to read through it, but it's too full of scientific details and difficult words. He's about to try another listing when he spots something halfway down the last page.

It's a place to send questions or comments.

Ben stares at it for a minute. Then he types:

I need help. There's a vernal pool with spadefoots in it near my house. The land is being sold and there is no place for the toads to go. How can I save them?

He puts his name in the box at the bottom, then adds his phone number.

He doesn't believe anyone will answer him. He's just a kid. *But so what,* he thinks. *They won't know this is from a kid!*

Just as he hits Send, his mother comes in the room.

"What are you doing?"

"Um, nothing. I'm trying to find out about vernal pools."

"What are they?"

"They're places where toads live. Like on Mrs. Tibbets's land."

"Ben, shouldn't you be finishing your desert report?"

"I know, I know."

"You take care of your homework, all right? Let Mrs. Tibbets take care of her toads." Ben looks back at his computer screen, and she finally leaves.

He glances over at the printer and pulls out the sheet of paper. The spadefoot in the photograph stares out at him. He can almost hear it calling.

"Here it is," Ben says, showing the picture in the book to Ryan and Jenny. "Here's the spadefoot."

Ryan bends over the page for a close look. "It's just a regular-looking old toad."

"It's kind of cute, though," Jenny says. "In a toadlike kind of way."

"I know they look regular, but there are hardly any left around here." Ben closes the book. "It was really cool to see them. There were all these toads in the pond swimming around, and they were all calling out. And Mrs. Tibbets and I were laughing about the Overtoad."

"The Overtoad?" Ryan blurts out. "What's that?"

"A huge toad with superpowers that looks after all the spadefoots."

"Is there really a big toad like that?" Ryan asks, hopping back and forth from one foot to the other.

"No, you dummy," Jenny says. "It's just a story."

"Yeah, but it sounded like it was there."

"I wish it was," said Ben. "We could use the Overtoad. Even here at school." He hands the book back to Ryan—it's almost time for school to start. "Here," he says, "You can take it back. Thanks. It was cool to look at."

"Did you see the blue poison dart frog?" Ryan asks. His eye that's not covered is dancing with excitement, as jumpy as the rest of him.

"Yeah, I did."

"And the one that looks like a leaf?"

"Yeah."

"And the one that has circles on its rear end that look like big eyes?"

"Yeah!" Ben says. "Like two cross-eyes. They were so funny!' He crosses his eyes, trying to look crazy. Suddenly a shadow of hurt passes over Ryan's face.

Jenny gives Ben a look, letting him know that he's made a big mistake.

"Thanks for giving the book back," Ryan says and turns away.

"Oh—Ryan, I wasn't making fun of you."

"I can't help it about my eye," Ryan says angrily. "I can't help it."

"Come on, Ryan. I don't care about your eye! I didn't—"

"I know you don't care," Ryan mutters.

"I meant—"

"Everyone to your seats," says Mrs. Kutcher, rapping on her desk with a pencil. "Time to get started."

Jenny sits down and turns to look at Ben. "I know you didn't mean it."

Ben rolls his eyes. "I'm an idiot."

"No," she says. "You're not an idiot. You are a little weird sometimes. But being weird is much better than being an idiot."

Ben shrugs. "Yeah, but what if you're an idiot who's weird, too?"

"Now that is a problem," Jenny says. "You might as well give up right now. Nothing worse than a weird idiot."

"I know." Ben nods. "I know."

Ben watches Ryan all through the morning, but Ryan avoids his gaze. At lunch Ben sits next to him, hoping to get him to smile, but Ryan just keeps his head down and doesn't say a word. After a few minutes, Frankie plops down across from them and promptly starts stealing french fries off other kids' plates. He stuffs the fries into his mouth, seeing how many he can get in at once. The boys around him guffaw. *If it wasn't Frankie's way of showing off,* Ben thinks, *it might actually be funny.* But even Frankie's french fry–packed mouth doesn't make Ryan smile.

When Frankie sees that neither Ryan nor Ben is laughing, he opens his mouth so everyone can see the mashed-up french fries. A few soggy bits spill out onto the table. Dennis Dimeo, Danny Martin, and Tommy Miller are laughing their heads off.

Frankie chews and swallows the huge lump of mushy potatoes, then looks at Ben and Ryan. Ben can see him trying to think of something to say.

"What's wrong with you, Captain Kidd?" Frankie finally says to Ryan.

"Lay off him," Ben says.

"Oh, excuse me," Frankie sneers. He glances at the other boys for support. "I didn't know you were Captain Kidd's bodyguard. Why don't you go chase frogs or something with Mrs. Ribbets?"

Everyone at the table looks at Ben, waiting to see what he'll say.

Frankie keeps going. "Mrs. Tibbets, Mrs. Ribbets. Ribbets Tibbets! Ribbets Tibbets!" He starts making frog noises. Kids are laughing again.

"Shut up, Frankie!" Jenny shouts from the other end of the table.

"What do you care? She's nothing but a dumb old science teacher."

Ben can't stand it anymore. "She's *not* dumb. She knows about a lot of things."

"Yeah. She's knows she's the worst teacher in the school."

"She's smart." Ben knows he's letting Frankie get to him. "She's cool."

Now even Ryan is looking at him like he's lost it. Who would ever call an old science teacher cool? But Ben can't stop himself. "You should see her yard and the woods on her property. And she's got all sorts of cool things around her house."

"What?" Frankie jeers. "Lots of flies for frogs to eat?'

"No, stupid. Animals...like snakes. Rattlesnakes. I've seen them."

"Right." Frankie rolls his eyes. "Rattlesnakes. Fat chance. What kind of old woman has rattlesnakes?"

Everyone at the table has stopped talking. All eyes are on Ben. He takes a quick look at Jenny. Her eyes are open wide—she can't believe what she's hearing. He wishes he hadn't said anything, but he can't back down now.

"It's true. She had two of them in a cage. She showed them to me."

That isn't exactly what happened, but he's sick of Frankie

making fun of everything everybody says. He wants to prove how great Mrs. Tibbets is—and how real the rattlesnakes are.

"Liar!" says Frankie.

"I am not."

"Liar," Frankie snarls again.

The word hits Ben hard. He stands up. "I swear it's true."

Suddenly Ryan stands up, too. "It's true. He told me he saw them!"

Ben is stunned. He's never said anything to Ryan about the rattlesnakes. He looks over, trying to figure out what's going on, but Ryan is staring hard at Frankie through his crazy glasses. Frankie's mouth opens like he's going to say something, but then it shuts again.

"Really?" Danny asks.

"Yeah, really," Ben says. Danny looks convinced. "And she let me see them," Ben insists. "But they got away and now they're out on her property."

He has no idea where the snakes are now. Mrs. Tibbets hadn't expected them to survive. But maybe they would. Maybe they're still alive.

"No way!" Frankie says, but this time his heart isn't in it. He looks around for support, but everyone's listening to Ben now.

"Uh-huh! It's true!" Ryan is shouting. "It's true!

"Oh, who cares about Mrs. Ribbets," Frankie says. He makes a face like this is all stupid and he doesn't care.

"Not only that," Ryan goes on. "The Overtoad will eat you up if you don't believe it!"

No one except Ben and Jenny has any idea what Ryan is talking about, and Jenny starts to laugh. Ben has to laugh, too, when he sees the bewildered look on Frankie's face. Frankie stares down at his plate. For once he can't think of anything to say.

Ben looks at Ryan and Ryan gives him a huge smile. When they head back to class, Ben catches up with Ryan and whispers in a dark, sinister voice, "Better look out for the Overtoad!"

"O-ver-toad! O-ver-toad!" Ryan chants. "Better look out for the Overtoad!"

Ben slips on his jacket and opens the back door.

"Where are you headed?" his mother asks.

"Just to walk out back," he says.

"I wanna come, too," Agatha says.

"Sorry," Ben says. "I need to go alone."

"Mom!" Agatha whines. "Tell Ben to let me go with him."

Mrs. Moroney narrows her eyes and studies Ben's face. "Let your brother go by himself this time," she says to Agatha. "Anyway, you have some work to do in your room."

"But, Mom—"

"You heard what I said, Agatha. And Ben, keep an eye on the time!" Ben remembers all the times she said that as he went out the garage door in Tucson, headed to the dry riverbed. He's not in Tucson anymore, but for just a moment, it feels the same.

The sun is shining, and in a minute Ben takes off his jacket and ties it around his waist. He walks along the trail through the marshy place he's come to know, stopping now and then to look at something that's just sprouting, or to listen for new sounds. Tiny leaves the size of cats' ears are opening on some of the maple trees. He turns over a log and finds a salamander, shiny black with bright yellow spots on its back. Very carefully he picks it up and holds it in his hand, then puts it down beside the log.

"You stay there," he says. He whistles to himself as he follows the trail toward Mrs. Tibbets's land. He pulls a folded sheet of paper out of his pocket. An official at the Natural Heritage Program actually answered his e-mail! He opens the printout and reads it again. "Thank you for your query," it says. "A member of our staff will give it careful attention and will get back to you as soon as possible." Ben smiles and puts the paper back in his pocket.

The trail widens a little, and the new leaves overhead

make little shadows on the ground. He's almost to the vernal pool when he hears men talking. He stops and peers through the trees. The men are wearing orange construction helmets, and they're carrying instruments on long tripods. Someone has tied orange plastic ribbons on a couple of tree trunks. In the distance Ben can see a truck, and he cuts toward it, stepping over fallen logs and wading through wet leaves. As he gets closer to the truck, the woods thin out and he comes into an open space. The street that runs in front of Mrs. Tibbets's house is not far away. Big white plastic tubes stick out of the ground in three or four places.

Ben's hands feel sweaty. He walks up to one of the men standing by the truck.

"What are you doing?" Ben asks.

"Surveying," the man answers. "Looks like they're planning to put up some houses here. We're measuring the lots."

"What are those plastic tubes for?" Ben asks.

"They're for something that's called a perc test," the man explains. "To make sure that the water can filter down into the soil. They can only build where the soil can drain properly."

Ben's heart leaps with hope. "What happens if the soil can't drain? Can they still build?"

"Oh, no worry about that. This land is too valuable. They'll find plenty of space for the houses. About a dozen of them."

"A dozen houses?"

"Yep." The man opens the door of the truck and takes out a thermos.

Ben turns away and retraces his steps back into the woods. He runs down the path and stops at the vernal pool.

He can't believe it. It's half the size it was that rainy night a week and a half ago. The edges of the pool are still muddy, layered with caked black leaves. But it's drying up fast, like a puddle on the sidewalk after a rainstorm.

Ben squishes over to its mucky edge and squats down. The water is murky, but he stays there a minute, watching and waiting.

Then he sees them.

At first he only makes out one or two darker shapes in the water, but then more come into focus. Dozens of tadpoles scurry around in the water, pumping with their hind legs, their little tails waving behind them.

Spadefoot tadpoles! Hundreds of them!

Ben takes off toward Mrs. Tibbets's house. When he sees her car in the driveway, he sprints around to the back of the house and looks through the window on the back door. Mrs. Tibbets is at the kitchen sink. He knocks. When she turns and sees him, her face breaks into a smile.

"Why, hello, Ben," she says as she opens the door. "What a nice surprise. Come on in. I think I can find a little something for us to snack on."

Ben takes off his muddy shoes and steps inside the

kitchen. He's not hungry. His mind is filled with what he just saw and what it means.

"Mrs. Tibbets, I saw the spadefoot tadpoles! There are lots of them!"

"Oh, I know," she says. "They're growing very quickly—they won't be in the pool very much longer. Another two weeks or so."

"And there are people out there measuring the land. They've put in these tubes to see if they can build houses."

"I know. I saw them when I came home."

"But aren't you going to do something?" Ben is pacing around the kitchen, unable to sit still. *How can she stand there so calmly?* he wonders.

"It's going to be all right," she says.

"What do you mean? The toads are going to be okay?"

Mrs. Tibbets hesitates for a minute before speaking. "Ben, I don't expect you to understand, but I explained the problem. My sister-in-law owns the land. She's going to sell it and the more I say about it, the worse it gets. I don't think we could prove the land is an endangered habitat anyway."

"But it is! We know it is! We have to try!"

Mrs. Tibbets has a pained look on her face. "I'm so sorry, Ben."

"Did you even call the people at the state?" Ben says. "I sent them an e-mail."

Mrs. Tibbets's eyes grow wide. "You did?"

"Yes, and I got an answer today. Look!" He pulls out the piece of paper and shows it to her.

"Well," says Mrs. Tibbets. "If Tabitha gets wind of this, she'll scream bloody murder."

"It wasn't you. I did it."

Mrs. Tibbets sighs. "Ben, it was very nice of you to try, but this is just a form letter. They probably send these notes to everyone who writes in."

"But they say they'll get back to me as soon as possible."

"I know you want to help, but I'm afraid there's nothing anyone can do now. Even if they did respond, by the time they came out here the pond may have dried up."

"You should have called them," he mutters as he turns to leave.

"Maybe. Maybe not. Everything will work out," Mrs. Tibbets calls to him. "You'll see."

Ben looks back at Mrs. Tibbets. He can tell by her face that she doesn't believe what she's saying. She's given up.

"Forget it," Ben says over his shoulder. He pulls his shoes on and stomps out the door and around the garage. As he rounds the corner near the garden, something makes him look back. The empty cage is still sitting under the lean-to. He pauses for a moment, then runs back and pounds on Mrs. Tibbets's door.

She pulls it open and looks at Ben in alarm. "What's wrong?" she asks.

"What about the timber rattlers? Maybe they're still out there. Wouldn't they be endangered if they're living there?"

Mrs. Tibbets shakes her head. "They're not there, Ben."

"But you're not sure! They could be. Maybe they survived and they've found a place to live around here. Then we'd have to let them be."

She shakes her head again. "I'm sure they're gone."

Ben knows she means they're dead. Neither of them can say the word. Dead. Gone.

"I have to go," Ben says. He turns toward the door.

"All right, Ben. Thanks for coming by. I'll see you in school."

Ben nods but doesn't look at her. He opens the door and leaves the house. He steals a glance behind him as he rounds the corner of the garage. Mrs. Tibbets is standing in the door watching him. She waves.

Ben heads down the path toward home. The sun is hot on his face, and he hears chickadees over his head as he passes into the woods. A blue jay brays out overhead, warning everything around that Ben is coming through. Little green shoots are coming up beside the path.

How can it be so beautiful on such a rotten day?

Chapter Thirteen

"Mr. Nickelby would like to see you in his office," Mrs. Kutcher says to Ben.

"He wants to see me?" Ben asks. "What for?"

"I don't know," she says. "The secretary just sent me a note asking for you to come to the principal's office. The last bell will ring in a few minutes, so you'd better get your things and hurry down there."

Ben walks down the empty hallway, wondering why Mr. Nickleby sent for him. He's never been called to the office for doing anything wrong before. He doesn't like Mr. Nickleby, but not just because he's the principal. Ben can't put his finger on why, but he just doesn't trust him.

Could I be in trouble because of my schoolwork? he wonders. He hasn't done his geography report, but Mr. Nickelby couldn't have heard about that. For all Mrs. Kutcher knows, he's been working on the report all along.

When he reaches the office, he sees his mom and dad just outside it, sitting in the chairs against the wall. *What are they doing here?* He gets a sick feeling in his stomach.

Before Ben can say anything to his parents, Mr. Nickelby strides out of his office toward them wearing one of those fake little smiles that adults give kids when they want something out of them.

"Hello, Ben," Mr. Nickelby says. "Why don't you all come on in?"

Ben looks at his parents for some sign, but their faces don't reveal anything.

"Come on, champ," his father says, smiling. But even his dad's smile isn't very comforting. Something is really wrong.

Mr. Nickelby gestures for them to come into his office. As Ben goes by, his mother reaches out and touches his shoulder. Mr. Nickelby drags in a couple of extra chairs so there's a place for each of them to sit. Then he positions himself behind his desk, like it's a fort or something.

Ben's mom pulls her chair close to Ben's.

What's wrong? Ben wonders. *Did something happen to Agatha? Is one of my grandparents sick?*

Mr. Nickelby leans back a little and folds his hands. "Ben, I asked your parents to come in so we could all talk about a couple of things—all of us here together. All right?"

"Sure." Ben's voice isn't much more than a squeak.

"How are you getting along with the kids in your class? Are you getting used to being here?"

"Um...sure," Ben says. "Yeah."

"Anybody in particular you're having a hard time with?"

"No, not really." He could do without Frankie Mirley and his buddies, and Ryan sometimes drives him crazy, but Ben's not about to say anything that would get anybody in trouble.

Mr. Nickelby pauses for a moment, scratching the side of his neck. Ben looks at his parents. They're trying to hide it, but he can tell they're upset. Finally his dad speaks.

"We've been talking with Mr. Nickleby while we were waiting for you. He'd like to ask you a few questions about Mrs. Tibbets."

"Okay," says Ben. This doesn't help much. He still can't figure out what's going on.

"How do you like Mrs. Tibbets?" Mr. Nickelby asks.

"Um...fine. I like her fine."

"I hear you've helped around her house a little."

"Uh-huh," Ben says. "Yes sir."

"What do you do when you go there?"

Now Ben is confused. He's sure there's a right answer and a wrong answer, but he can't think of what they might be or where this conversation is headed. It feels like a trap. "I helped in her backyard, and one night she showed me some toads in a little pool."

All three adults stare at Ben. Mr. Nickelby breaks the uncomfortable silence with another question. "Anything else?"

"No," Ben says, shaking his head.

Mr. Nickelby draws in a breath. "What about snakes? Did you help her with snakes?"

"No."

Did Mrs. Tibbets tell Mr. Nickelby about how he let the snakes out? Is he in trouble for that?

"Does Mrs. Tibbets have some poisonous snakes? Rattlesnakes, for instance?"

Ben glances over at his parents. His dad's sitting there, looking like he's trying his best to keep his mouth shut. His mom just looks worried.

"Couldn't you ask her?" Ben doesn't want to say more until he figures out what's going on.

"I'll talk to Mrs. Tibbets. But first we'd like to hear your story."

"Ben?" His dad's eyes look tired. "Just tell Mr. Nickelby what you know."

"Well, she did, but they got away."

"Did she let you help with the snakes?" Mr. Nickleby asks.

"No, not really."

"What do you mean, not really? Did she let you get near them?"

"No, she—"

"Well, Ben," Mr. Nickelby interrupts. "Here's the problem. That's not what you told some other kids."

"I know, but...but that was just a story I made up."

"But we understand that Ryan Brisson said it was true."

Suddenly Ben's dad sits forward. "Wait a minute, Mr. Nickleby. We've talked about this already. The snakes got away—Mrs. Tibbets called us and told us. Ben doesn't know anything about it."

Ben glances over at his dad. His parents trust him, but they don't know what really happened.

"I want Ben's side of the story," Mr. Nickleby said.

"Ryan didn't know anything about it. He was just saying that so the other kids would believe me. He's never even been to her house. "

Mr. Nickelby leans forward. "So you didn't have anything to do with the snakes?"

Ben looks at his parents. He bows his head.

"What is it, Ben?" his mother asks.

"What happened, Ben?" his father asks. Now they're both concerned.

"I let them out," Ben whispers.

"What did you say?" Mr. Nickleby asks. "I didn't hear you."

"I let them out," Ben says, louder. "I didn't mean to, but I did."

"Ben," his mother says, "you told us you didn't!"

"I know. I'm sorry."

"Did Mrs. Tibbets know you opened the cage?" Mr. Nickleby asks.

"No. I didn't tell her. She told me not to touch the cage. But I did. And they got out."

"Ben, why didn't you tell us?" his mom asks.

"I couldn't. I wanted to. But I couldn't. And then finally I told Mrs. Tibbets—the night of the spadefoots. She wasn't—"

"Mrs. Tibbets should have told you," Mr. Nickleby said to Ben's parents. "And she shouldn't have left Ben alone with the snakes."

Suddenly Ben understands. Mr. Nickleby isn't mad at him. He's mad at Mrs. Tibbets. "She told me not to!" Ben tries to keep his voice under control. "I wasn't supposed to go near them. It wasn't her fault! She told me not to go near the snakes, and I did it anyway."

"All right," says Mr. Nickelby, shifting in his chair. "I think I've got a pretty good picture of what happened."

"No, you don't!" Ben protests.

"Okay, okay," Ben's dad says. He puts his hand on the back of Ben's neck and gives it a gentle squeeze.

"It's all right, Ben," says Mr. Nickelby. "We don't need to talk about this any more right now." He relaxes back into his chair. "What about your classes? Any problems there?"

Ben shakes his head.

"I hear the fifth graders are doing a big report on ecosystems. How's yours coming?"

"Okay." Ben can't get his mind off the snakes. Why didn't he just leave the cage alone? And why did he have to tell stupid Frankie Mirley about them?

Everybody stands up. Mr. Nickelby extends his hand for Ben to shake. Ben doesn't want to, but he forces himself to put out his hand. The principal's palm is moist with sweat.

"Will Mrs. Tibbets be okay?" Ben asks.

"We'll see how things work out," Mr. Nickelby says.

"It really wasn't her fault. She—"

"I know that's what you think, Ben." Mr. Nickelby guides him toward the door. "Why don't you step outside and let me talk with your parents for just a minute?"

Ben waits just outside the office, listening. He can hear Mr. Nickleby's voice, but he can't make out the words. Just as school lets out, Ben grabs his backpack and dashes down the hallway, dodging between the kids pouring out of the classrooms.

He runs all the way to Mrs. Tibbets's room.

She's not there.

Chapter Fourteen

Ben slumps down in the backseat of the car. Agatha sits beside him, chattering a blue streak. For once he's grateful for her mouth. He looks out the window. The leaves on the trees are opening, and the lawns and fields are turning a soft yellow green. He opens the window a crack. The air is warmer than it was yesterday. He thinks about the vernal pool and wonders if it has shrunk even more.

When they get home, his father stands by the front door as Ben's mom and sister walk in. Ben tries to slip by him, but his father catches his arm.

"Ben—"

Ben stops and looks up at his father.

"Ben, you've never lied to us before."

His father isn't yelling. He'd rather have him yell.

"I didn't lie," Ben says. "I just didn't tell you."

"Same difference," his father says. "You should have told us. You hurt me and your mom."

"I know," Ben says. "It was too hard."

"Well, look where we are now. It's much worse than if you had told us."

Ben nods. It's true.

"And Mrs. Tibbets made a mistake, too."

"Dad, don't blame her. Mr. Nickleby doesn't like her."

"I can see that. She may be a good person. And a great teacher, but still..."

"She is," Ben says.

They both stand there in the doorway. Finally his dad shakes his head and says, "Well, we'll all learn something from this. Why don't you go do your homework now? I have to get back to work. I'll see you at dinner."

Back in his room, Ben sits at his desk and stares at the wall. Pretty soon, his mind is back on Mrs. Tibbets's land and the spadefoots. He's made everything worse, somehow.

The Overtoad would know what to do. For starters, he could swallow Mr. Nickleby and Mrs. Tibbets's sister-in-law and the men with the bulldozers.

Ben rummages through his backpack looking for the

sheet about the ecosystems report. Only one week left. If he starts on it now, there'll still be time.

Amphibians of the World is sitting on his desk. Ben drops his backpack and leafs through the book, skipping over the Amazon rain forest and Central America until he comes to North America. He flips past the pictures of the tree frogs and leopard frogs and the enormous Rocky Mountain toad. When he comes to the picture of the Colorado River toad, he remembers the one that sat in their laundry room in Tucson. *Boy, that was a long time ago,* he thinks. Then he turns the page and there it is, the eastern spadefoot.

It's not fancy like the leopard frog. Or big like the Rocky Mountain toad.

Nobody will miss it when it's gone.

He thinks about Mrs. Tibbets. Could she lose her job all because of a couple of rattlesnakes? If she does, it will be his fault.

He thinks about Ryan. His friend stuck with him at lunch, in spite of Ben's stupid comment about the crossed eyes. Ben smiles, thinking about Ryan's attempt to stand up for him. Poor, goofy Ryan. Even when he's trying to help, things go wrong.

The phone rings, and he slams the book shut. Another ring. *Mom and Agatha must be outside,* he thinks.

He picks up on the fourth ring. "Hello." A man's voice at the other end of the line says, "I'm calling for Ben Moroney."

"That's me," Ben answers. "I'm Ben."

"Oh," the man says, sounding a little confused. "Is your dad named Ben, too?"

"No, just me."

"Well, Ben, this is Hank Lindsey from the Natural Heritage Program at the state division of Fisheries and Wildlife. I got an e-mail from you about some spadefoot toads."

For a second Ben is speechless. He can't believe it. But when he starts speaking, he can't stop. "Yes sir. Thanks for calling back, Mr. Lindsey. Thanks so much. Really. My teacher Mrs. Tibbets has spadefoots in her vernal pool and her sister-in-law wants to sell the land and I was wondering if you could save it."

"Whoa," the man says. "Hold on. Whose land is it?"

Ben struggles for the best way to tell the story. "Well, part of it belongs to my teacher—the part where her house is—but the rest of it belongs to her sister-in-law, and now that my teacher's husband died, her sister-in-law wants to sell the property so they can build houses there. But the spadefoot toads have already hatched out in the vernal pool. And I think maybe there's some salamanders, too. Spadefoots are endangered, aren't they? I tried to figure out how to stop them from bulldozing the pond, but I didn't know what to do. So I thought if you could just come and see..."

It's all Ben can think of to say. It's quiet on the other end of the line for a few seconds, then the man says, "Well, I don't know..."

"Please," Ben begs. "Just come and look at it. It's really beautiful. We found fifteen pairs of spadefoots. No, sixteen."

"You're sure they were spadefoots?"

"They're smoother than other toads, and they've got these little pads on their hind feet...and yellow stripes on their backs. Oh, and their pupils are vertical, and—"

"Okay, okay." The man chuckles. "I believe you. And how did you find them?"

"Mrs. Tibbets took me to the pond."

"You went out looking for them?"

"Uh-huh. A couple of weeks ago, when it rained really hard one night."

"I know the night. I was out, too."

"You were?"

"I sure was. Ben, if you don't mind my asking, how old are you?"

"Ten, almost eleven."

"And this is your teacher's land?"

"Right. It's Mrs. Tibbets's—and her sister-in-law's."

"I—wait a minute. Is this Mrs. Tibbets, the wife of Tom Tibbets? The high school teacher?"

"Yes sir. Her husband's name was Thomas. But he died a year ago."

"Oh, I hadn't heard. I knew him. He was a good scientist."

"So is Mrs. Tibbets."

Ben notices that his mother has come into the room. He gives her a pleading look so she doesn't interrupt.

"Can you come?" Ben asks.

"Well, son, I don't know how much I can do. It sounds pretty complicated."

"I know, sir. But you've got to help us. They're going to start building soon and this is our last chance."

"I know you want to save the spadefoots, but it's the ownership of the land that's a problem. And if the pool is very small and dries up before we get a chance to document it, it will be difficult to certify it as endangered habitat. Listen, why don't you give me Mrs. Tibbets's phone number and I'll give her a call."

"But can you come? Soon, I mean?" Ben hears the man leafing through some papers.

"I'm in Boston at meetings most of the week, and I have to be in the field all day Thursday. I could try to come Friday."

"Can't you come sooner?"

"I'm sorry, Friday will have to do. Don't get your hopes up too much, Ben. There's got to be definite documentation to hold up something like a building project."

"Okay," says Ben. "But please come."

"Ben, did Mrs. Tibbets teach you about those spadefoots?"

"Yes sir."

"She must be a good teacher."

"She is."

Ben finds Mrs. Tibbets's number where his mom had written it on the cover of their telephone book and reads it out. He says good-bye and hangs up.

His mother is still standing there, staring at him. "Ben, honey, what on earth is going on?"

"That was a man named Mr. Lindsey. He's from the Natural Heritage Program."

"Natural Heritage? What did he want?"

"He's going to try to help us save Mrs. Tibbets's land."

"I don't know what you're talking about, honey."

Ben starts to explain. "Mrs. Tibbet's sister-in-law owns the land with the pool on it. She want to sell it and I thought—"

His mother interrupts, "Ben, you're only in fifth grade. This has got to stop. You've already caused enough trouble with Mrs. Tibbets and her snakes. You need to do homework and play with friends and let grown-ups worry about problems like this. You can't interfere in other people's business."

"But if the man comes and looks at the land—"

"No, listen to me. That's enough, Ben. Mrs. Tibbets is a grown-up. This is her problem. You have to stay out of it."

Ben knows there's no use arguing. "Okay, Mom. Okay."

His mother looks at him. "That doesn't sound very convincing. I'm thinking your dad and I will have to have a talk with Mrs. Tibbets. Maybe her sister-in-law is right. Maybe she should sell the land. I still can't imagine what she was thinking, keeping those snakes—"

"Please don't call her, Mom."

His mother shakes her head and goes into the kitchen. "We'll need to talk this over more when your father gets home," she calls.

Ben can't wait. He has to see Mrs. Tibbets. He has to see her *now.*

He slips on his boots and jacket. As he's going out the back door, he yells back, "I'm gonna take a little walk. I'll be back soon."

"Ben!" his mother yells. "Wait!"

But he's out the door and across the backyard, heading quickly toward Mrs. Tibbets's on the path through the marsh.

A path he knows by heart.

Chapter Fifteen

Mrs. Tibbets's car isn't in the driveway. Ben knocks on the door. No answer. He goes around the house and peers through the kitchen window. She isn't home.

He runs back around the garage, then takes the trail back to the vernal pool. It's barely ten feet across now—not much more than a big puddle. He hunkers down to look for the tadpoles, but he can't see any. He pushes the muddy leaves around with a stick, hoping to stir them up.

Are they gone already? How can he save the land if there aren't any endangered animals here? He's pretty sure he convinced Mr. Lindsey there had been spadefoots in the pool, but he doubts that will be enough. He doubles back through the woods and checks the house again. Now Mrs. Tibbets is in the backyard filling some bird feeders.

"Hi, Mrs. Tibbets," Ben calls, hoping his nervousness doesn't show in his voice.

"Oh, hi, Ben. Can you help me? This bag is so big I can barely lift it."

Ben goes over and takes one corner of the bag and together they fill the rest of the feeders. "I tried to find you after school," Ben says.

"Oh? Sorry I missed you. I had a meeting."

Ben's mouth goes dry, but he makes himself say it. "I told Mr. Nickleby and my parents you didn't let me near the rattlesnakes. I told them everything was my fault."

"No. It was all my fault. I never should have kept the snakes. I should have had someone take them away as soon as Thomas died. But I knew he was so fond of them..." She laughs. "Fond of rattlesnakes—there aren't many people you can say that of."

"Still, you told me to stay away from the cage. If I had done what you said, they never would've gotten loose." Ben helps Mrs. Tibbets carry the bag to the garage. "Are you going to lose your job?" he asks.

"Ben, I'm going to tell you something. I used to look forward to going to school each day. But I don't think I should teach anymore. There's too much red tape for me now, too many forms to fill out and too many meetings. I like being with children. I like science. I like teaching. But I don't like school anymore."

"I wouldn't want to teach either, if I had to work for Mr. Nickelby," Ben says. Mrs. Tibbets doesn't respond, but he can see the hint of a smile in her eyes. "I talked to a man from the state," he says. "About the spadefoots. He said he would call you."

"I know," said Mrs. Tibbets.

"You know?"

"He called just as I got home."

"Is he coming?"

"Yes, he's coming. But I don't think it will do any good, Ben. When I explained the situation, he said it didn't look good. Just as I thought."

"But maybe," Ben says.

"Maybe," Mrs. Tibbets repeats. "Maybe. But I think he's only coming as a favor because he knew my husband. Unfortunately I think my sister-in-law and the real estate agent will be here, too."

"Why do they have to come?"

"It's Tabitha's land, Ben, not mine."

"Well, if she owns the land, then she owns the spadefoots. And if she owns the spadefoots, she should take care of them. They were here first."

Mrs. Tibbets looks up in the sky. "I wonder," she says, "what toads would do if they owned the land and we lived on it?"

Ben pictures the Overtoad looking down on them, deciding what would happen to people. "I think we'd be in big trouble," he says.

"I think you're right," says Mrs. Tibbets. They're quiet for a minute, then she asks, "Do your parents know you're here?"

"No, not really."

"Maybe you should go home now. We're all in enough hot water. They must think I'm a weird old woman."

"No, they don't."

"Well, that's what I am. An odd old duck in hiking boots. Now shoo!"

Ben gives her a little nod and heads for home. *Why won't she do anything to try and save her land?* he wonders. He wants to be mad at her, but he can't. He picks up his pace—he doesn't want to be late for dinner.

Mrs. Tibbets is right about one thing: he's already in enough trouble. Maybe his parents should just wrap him up and stick him in a box and ship him back to Tucson.

Chapter Sixteen

Did you know the ice fish in the Antarctic Ocean have their own antifreeze? If they didn't, they'd be ice cubes. And did you know it gets so cold down there that your skin would freeze in only a minute?"

Ben tries to look interested, but to tell the truth he's sick of hearing about Ryan's geography report. The bus stops and a few kids get off. Ryan babbles on about Antarctic skuas and Adélie penguins. Ben is wondering how much longer it will take the bus to reach school when he hears a low chant coming from the back of the bus. Someone laughs. The chant gets louder. Ben can't make out the words, but he can tell that more kids have joined in. He turns around.

Frankie Mirley is in the back of the bus, leading the boys in the backseats in a dumb, singsongy chorus: "Captain Kidd and Snakeman...Captain Kidd and Snakeman...Captain Kidd and Snakeman..."

Ryan has finally heard it, too. "Frankie's such a jerk!" he mutters to Ben. Before Ben can stop him, Ryan stands up in the aisle and shouts in the same singsong way, "Frankie's such a jerk...Frankie's such a jerk..." He yells even louder than Frankie, and the kids on the front of the bus stop talking and turn around.

When the bus slows down for the next stop, Frankie makes his way up the aisle and pushes Ryan back into his seat. "Say that again, matey," he says, holding one hand over his eye like a patch.

Ben's heart pounds. "Stop it!" he says.

"Oh, look. Snakeman can talk!" Frankie turns around to make sure the other boys are watching. He makes a rattling sound with his mouth: "*Chakachakachaka.*"

"Leave Ryan alone," says Ben. "You started it with that stupid chant."

"What do you say, Cap'n? Do you want me to leave you alone?" Frankie tries to yank Ryan's glasses off, but Ben knocks his hand away. The glasses with the patch hang lopsided halfway down Ryan's nose.

Ben has had it. Without thinking, he climbs over Ryan and lifts Frankie up by his jacket, pushing him back down the aisle.

"Hey!" the bus driver shouts. "Enough of that. Everyone in your seats!"

Suddenly everyone is yelling and hooting.

"Leave him alone!" Ben screams. "Leave my friend alone!" Ben's eyes fill with tears, but he doesn't care if anyone sees. He gives Frankie's jacket another shake and shoves him back in his seat.

The bus driver pulls the bus to the curb and lurches down the aisle. "You boys settle down or you'll be walking to school for the next month!"

Everyone on the bus is quiet now. Ben drops down in the seat next to Frankie. "Sorry," he says to the driver.

"I'd better not hear another word out of you two." The bus driver glares at them, then returns to the front.

As soon as the bus pulls away from the curb, Frankie snorts in disgust. "I'm glad I'm moving. This school and all the losers in it like you stink big-time."

"You're moving?" Ben can't believe what he just heard. "You're leaving? When?"

"This summer," Frankie says. "I wish it was tomorrow. Who wants to live in this crappy town, anyway?"

Ben tries to hide a smile. "Good luck."

"What do you mean?" Frankie says.

"I mean good luck being the new kid in a different school. You'd better hope that wherever you move, the kids there are nicer than you. Because you can be a real creep."

"Yeah!" Ryan is up on his knees, looking over the back of the seat. "I hope the Overtoad eats you up!"

Danny Martin chokes back a laugh. Frankie glowers at him, and Danny whirls around to face the front.

At the next bus stop Ben heads back to his seat. "One for the Overtoad," he says to Ryan.

"Yeah, one for the Overtoad." Ryan gives Ben a huge, goofy grin and picks up his backpack. "Gotta get off here, but I'll see ya tomorrow," he says. "We'll have a blast."

"See you, Ryan." Ben watches out the window as Ryan gets off the bus and heads across the street to his house. Ben is still shaky inside from the encounter with Frankie, but he grins. He can feel people looking at him, but it doesn't bother him at all.

Then he remembers his geography report. His stomach rolls over once, then settles into a dull churning.

"Hey." His father is standing at the door of Ben's room. Agatha is beside him, already in her pajamas.

"Hey," Ben says, placing his arm over the notes and desert pictures scattered on his desk.

"How's the report?"

"Pretty good," Ben says, hoping that will be enough for his father.

His dad plops down on Ben's bed and pulls Agatha onto his lap. Ben cringes. This is not good.

"Your mom thought maybe we ought to take a look at it and see if we can help you finish it up."

"No, that's okay," Ben says. "I can do it."

"Actually, I'd like to see it."

It's quiet for a couple of seconds. Ben points to the papers on the desk. "Here it is."

"Those look like notes. Can I see what you've written?"

"I haven't really written much yet," Ben mutters. He fumbles for something else to say, knowing the truth is about to come out. To make matters worse, his mom sticks her head in the door.

"Bedtime," she says.

"Ben's showing Dad his report," Agatha says, "except he doesn't have it."

Ben gives his sister a hard look. "Why don't you go jump in a lake," he says.

"Because I don't want to," Agatha says. "You're the one who's in—"

"Agatha, enough!" Dad lifts her off his lap and puts her on the floor. "Have you written *anything*, Ben?"

"Um...not much."

"Ben, you told us you were working on it and we trusted you," his dad says. "Haven't you even started writing?"

Ben shrugs.

"Uh-oh," Agatha says. "Now Ben's in trouble in a bunch of ways."

"Shut up, Agatha!" Ben wants to strangle his little sister.

"What do you mean 'a bunch of ways'?" his mom asks.

"Should I tell them?" Agatha keeps her eyes on Ben but edges closer to her mother.

"No!" Ben says.

"Okay, okay, okay," says their father. "What's happening?"

"Ben got in a fight and almost got thrown off the bus."

"I did not!"

"Did so. The bus driver says you're not supposed to fight on the bus and you did."

"Agatha!" Ben yells.

"Enough! Enough!" their father says. "Agatha, go with Mom."

Agatha sticks her tongue out at Ben as Mom drags her out the door.

"Ben, what is going on with you?"

There's so much going on in his head, Ben doesn't know where to start.

"Is this about Mrs. Tibbets?" his dad asks. "Is that why you're not doing your work?"

"No!" Actually it *is* about Mrs. Tibbets, but it's also about Frankie and Ryan and the spadefoots and Mrs. Tibbets's sister-in-law and the man from the Natural Heritage Program. And being new.

His father sits on the bed holding his head in his hands and staring at the floor.

"Sorry, Dad," Ben says.

His father looks up. "What are you going to do about your report? It's Wednesday, and isn't it due on Friday?"

"I'll finish it tomorrow," Ben says.

"Just make sure you get it done." His father stands and comes over to Ben's chair. "Is there anything I can do to help?"

Ben shakes his head.

"I love you, pal," his dad says.

"I know," Ben says. "Thanks."

It's torture getting through classes the next morning. Every time Ben thinks about the report, his stomach clenches up.

While Mrs. Kutcher is writing something on the board, Jenny turns around in her seat. "I heard about the fight!" she whispers.

"It wasn't a fight," Ben says.

"It sure sounded like a fight. I notice Mr. Loudmouth is pretty quiet this morning."

Ben looks back toward Frankie's desk. Frankie is staring straight at him, but he jerks his head down the moment Ben meets his gaze.

Ben doesn't really care about Frankie. He's got more important things on his mind. The pool in the woods behind Mrs. Tibbets's house is surely gone by now. But he'll just have to stop worrying about that problem and hope he and Mrs. Tibbets can convince Mr. Lindsey that there really were spadefoots in the pool.

Now he needs to concentrate on his report. He can get more stuff off the Internet, and after school he can go to the town library. He can even ask his mom or dad for help. He could draw a map of the area. Maybe he can pull it off. He feels better. He can do it.

Ben crams his books and his desert note cards into his backpack. It's almost time for dismissal.

"Hey, Ben," Jenny says, looking back over her shoulder.

"Yeah?"

"See you this afternoon."

"What for?"

"You know. Ryan's party."

"What?"

"Today is Ryan's party. I know he invited you. You're coming, right?"

Ben remembers the party hat invitation he stuffed under the papers in his desk. He feels like he might throw up.

"Is your mom bringing you over?"

"Um...I don't know," Ben stammers. "I-I guess so."

"Okay then. See you there." Jenny disappears into the crowd of kids leaving the classroom.

Ryan sits next to Ben on the bus. He's so excited about his party, he's talking even faster than usual. Ben smiles like he's listening, but his mind is all over the place, trying to figure out what to do.

Ben finally interrupts the nonstop chatter. "Ryan?"

"Yeah?"

"I can't come today."

"What?"

"I'm sorry. I can't come to your party. I haven't done my report. I'm pretty much grounded until I finish it. I'm really sorry."

"But...but you said you were coming. You said my mom didn't need to call."

"I know. I *was* coming. I totally forgot it was today. And if I don't get this report done, I'll be in big trouble."

"You've been working on it for weeks. Can't you just finish it after the party?"

"I can't. I've barely even started on it."

"But my mom has already ordered the pizza and everything!"

"That's okay. There'll be more for everybody else. Come on, Ryan. I said I'm sorry. You'll have plenty of fun without me."

Ryan turns his back to Ben and stares out the window. When the bus pulls up to Ryan's stop, he squeezes past Ben and trudges down the aisle.

Ben watches him as he steps onto the sidewalk. Ryan takes off his glasses and rubs his shirtsleeve across his eyes. He glances up at the bus window. His lazy eye looks off to the left, like he's watching someone in the street. But the other one looks straight at Ben, hurt and sad.

At his stop, Ben climbs down from the bus and walks toward his house. Agatha trails along behind him. "I know something you don't know," she sings. "I know something you don't know."

Ben tries to ignore her, but she sings it louder and louder. Finally Ben turns to face her. "Okay already. I give up. What do you know that I don't know?"

"It's about Ryan's party," she says.

"What?"

"Rory told me that you and Jenny are the only ones he invited. She says you're his only real friends."

"That's not true," Ben says.

"Yes it is," she says. "It's a secret."

"I'm going to the library to work on my report," Ben tells his mom.

"Don't you want a ride?" she asks, looking up from her magazine.

"No thanks. I'm taking my bike. It's not too far."

"Okay," she says. "Work hard."

Ben slips his backpack over his shoulders, climbs on his bike, and pedals out of the driveway. Ten minutes later he pulls up into Ryan's driveway and leaves his bike on the grass. When he knocks on the door, Rory opens it. "Ryan! Jenny!" she screams. "Ryan! Ben's here!"

Ben hears someone running. He reaches in his backpack and pulls out *Amphibians of the World.*

Ryan pushes Rory out of the way and swings the door wide open.

"Happy birthday," Ben says, holding out the book.

Ryan's smile is so big it seems like it's going to fall off his face. "Cool," he says. "Cool. This is so cool!"

Ben peers through the kitchen window. His father is pacing back and forth, something he does when he's excited or upset. His mother is leaning against the counter with her arms folded.

Ben takes a deep breath and opens the back door.

"Is that you, Ben?" his mother asks.

"Yeah," Ben calls, waiting for the ax to fall.

"Where on earth have you been? I was ready to send your father out looking for you!"

"I've been at Ryan's house."

"Ryan's house? You said you were going to the library."

"I know."

"Ben," his father says. "You lied to your mother."

"I know. I'm sorry."

"You were supposed to be working on your report."

"But I had to go to Ryan's party. I promised him I would."

"And why didn't we know about this party?" his mother asks.

"I forgot to tell you."

His parents look at each other like their son has lost his mind.

His father shakes his head, then squeezes the bridge of his nose with his fingers. "Go work on your report. We'll talk about your punishment tomorrow," his father says.

"But, Dad—"

"But, nothing. Go to your room and get busy. Now. I don't know where all this lying is coming from, but it's going to stop."

Ben's cheeks are hot. He doesn't blame his parents for being mad, but he was only trying to do the right thing.

"Dad!" Agatha bursts into the kitchen. Ben is about to tell her to get out, but he stops when he sees her face—all red and in a pout. She plants herself in the middle of the room, arms folded across her chest. "I heard what you said. It's not fair," she says. "Ben was just being a friend."

"That's enough, Agatha," Dad says. "This doesn't have—"

"Why are you punishing Ben? He messed up by not doing his report sooner, but Ryan doesn't have any friends besides Ben and Jenny. And isn't being a friend more important than finishing a dumb report?"

Ben stares at his sister, not sure he heard her right.

"Ben has to make friends if he's going to live here. All his other friends are in Tucson," Agatha says.

His parents are looking at each other again. His father's mouth is all twisted, like he's trying not to smile. His mother looks away, like she doesn't want anyone to see what she's thinking.

Agatha, the twitty little sister, breaks through the parent barrier? Ben thinks. *It's a miracle.*

"Well,"—his mother clears her throat—"even if that's true, you still have to do your report. You promised you'd get it done tonight."

Somehow, in the smallest of ways, twitty Agatha has given Ben a little breathing space.

"Okay," he says. As he walks past his mom and dad, he can feel their eyes on him. When he passes Agatha, he motions for her to follow him. They walk down the hall together. At the door to his room, Ben turns and looks into his little sister's eyes.

"Thanks, Agatha," he says. "Thanks a lot. You saved my butt in there."

"I know," she says. "I'm a good saver."

"Bring your reports up, please. Wait until I call your row." Mrs. Kutcher stands at the front of the class and watches as her students file up and place their reports on the big table under the bulletin board. "Thank you, class. I appreciate all your hard work, and I look forward to reading each one. Now I'd like you to sit silently for a few minutes and read tomorrow's assignment, pages 178 to 190."

When everyone is reading quietly, Mrs. Kutcher motions for Ben to come up to her desk.

"I didn't see you hand in a report, Ben. Did you forget and leave yours at home?"

"I didn't finish," Ben says, keeping his head down.

"Why not? I gave the assignment weeks ago."

Ben shrugs. "I just couldn't get it done."

"If you needed more time, why didn't you come to me sooner?" Mrs. Kutcher leans on her desk. "Well, what are we going to do?"

"Maybe I could do it this weekend?"

"That doesn't sound very convincing."

Suddenly Ryan is at Ben's side. "Mrs. Kutcher," he begins.

His voice is too loud, like always. Other kids can hear him. It's embarrassing, but it's too late to stop him—not that anyone could stop him anyway. "Ben wanted to do his paper. But he had to come to my party."

Mrs. Kutcher eyes Ryan, then looks back at Ben.

Jenny appears on the other side of the teacher's desk. "It's true, Mrs. Kutcher. Ben promised he would go to the party, and when he said he couldn't come because he had to do his report, Ryan was really disappointed."

Mrs. Kutcher looks at all of them, then stares out the window for a moment, chewing on her bottom lip. Ben can't tell what she's thinking.

"Ryan, Jenny, please go sit down," she finally says.

"Okay, but—" Ryan starts.

"Sit down, Ryan," Mrs. Kutcher repeats.

"Okay, okay," Ryan says.

Mrs. Kutcher waits until Ryan and Jenny are in their seats, then looks back at Ben. "You've known about this report for a long, long time. You even showed me some of your notes."

"I know."

"Why didn't you finish it?"

"I don't know."

"There must be some reason. You're so fascinated with the desert, and you already know so much about it."

"I guess I've been doing other things. And the desert just isn't as interesting to me as I thought it was."

"Why didn't you say something?"

"I don't know. I kept thinking I'd get the report done."

Mrs. Kutcher is quiet for a moment, then says, "If you could pick another ecosystem, what would it be?"

Ben is afraid to say "I don't know" again. He stares at his feet.

"I have an idea," the teacher says, and Ben looks up. He can tell by the tone of her voice it's something new, something different. "Why don't you write about a habitat around here? You're new in Massachusetts, and it might be interesting for you to find out about your new environment."

Ben is astounded. Mrs. Kutcher knows more about him than he thought she did. Could she have been talking to Mrs. Tibbets?

"Like what?" he asks.

"Well, what do *you* think?"

"Wetlands maybe? Swamps and ponds and marshes?"

"Sounds good to me," she says, and smiles.

"Okay." He'll have to start all over, but at least she's giving him a second chance.

"And since you've changed topics, why don't I give you a week? It's still a lot of work to do in that time."

"That's great," says Ben. He feels the relief wash over him.

"All right. One week. That's it. And remember, I'll have to deduct points because you didn't get it in on time."

"Okay, thanks. Thanks!" Ben rushes back to his desk

before she can change her mind. Jenny's looking at him with an eager gleam in her eyes.

"What happened?"

"She's taking off points, but she's giving me another week. I'm going to do my report on ponds and swamps here in Massachusetts."

Jenny holds up her hand for a high five.

Chapter Seventeen

When Ben gets home he grabs a snack and is about to head back outside when his mom calls out, "There's something for you in your room." He runs down the hall and finds a big box sitting on his bedroom floor. Its corners are squashed and Ben recognizes his own handwriting on the side—BEN'S ROOM.

"Finally," he says to himself. He drops his backpack, rips the tape off the box, and pulls back on the flaps. His mom comes in and leans against the door, watching him.

His first thought when he looks in the box is that there's not as much stuff as he remembered. What's missing? He pulls out the little pill bottles holding insects. The plastic food container that holds the snakeskin. The posters of desert animals he folded so carefully when he packed in Tucson. And finally, down at the bottom, the books and his collection of rocks.

"Happy?" his mother asks.

"Yeah," Ben says.

His mother smiles and leaves the room. Ben looks through the stuff again. It's all there. But it still feels like something is missing. It's not as exciting or comforting as he thought it would be. All of the things in the box seem like parts of his life from so long ago. Some other time. Some other place. He's glad he got the box back, but it doesn't seem so important now. He puts the stuff back in the box and runs to the kitchen.

His mom is busy with something on the other side of the room, so Ben grabs a handful of cookies and heads outside.

He thinks about going by the trail, but decides his bike will be faster. He wants to get to Mrs. Tibbets's house before anyone else does. But by the time he gets there, the driveway is filled with cars. Mrs. Tibbets's old station wagon sits next to her sister-in-law's car. Parked behind them are a bright green van with the name of a real estate company on the side and a blue car with a state insignia on the door.

Ben's heart races. He knocks on the front door. When nobody answers, he walks around to the back and finds four people standing in a semicircle, looking at the back field. Sandwiched between Mrs. Tibbets and her sister-in-law are a tall lady in a business suit with a purse slung over her shoulder and a short, stocky man in a brown windbreaker, an ancient green baseball cap, and hiking boots. He's holding a clipboard under one arm. No one's talking.

They're just standing there looking like they'd rather be somewhere else.

They all turn when they hear Ben come up.

"Hello, Ben," says Mrs. Tibbets.

"Hi," Ben says back.

"This is Tabitha Turner, my sister-in-law, and this is Adela Garrett, her real estate agent. And this—"

"You must be the young man who called," says the man in the green cap. His face breaks into a grin. "I'm Hank Lindsey," he says, holding out his hand. Ben's dad has always told him you can tell a lot from someone's handshake, and Ben likes the friendly way Hank Lindsey shakes his hand.

"Hi, Mr. Lindsey."

The real estate agent looks at Ben and Mr. Lindsey like she thinks they don't belong here. But Ben isn't leaving. Not now.

Then Mrs. Tibbets's sister-in-law speaks up. "Excuse me, but I'm still mystified as to why this boy felt free to invite a person from the state onto my property."

"I spoke with Mr. Lindsey, too, Tabitha," Mrs. Tibbets says. "I told him he should come."

Tabitha Turner sniffs and shakes her head.

"Well," says Mrs. Garrett, "this is certainly a beautiful piece of property. It has terrific possibilities." She gives Hank Lindsey a tight little smile. There's an awkward moment of silence, and Ben is glad he doesn't have to do anything but stand there and be a kid.

"Well," Mr. Lindsey says, taking out his clipboard. "Let's go have a look."

"It's over here," says Mrs. Tibbets. "The pool is down the path on the other side of the garage." She leads the way and everyone follows behind her in a straggly line.

"What was in there?" Mr. Lindsey asks, nodding to the empty cages beside the garage.

"Snakes," says Mrs. Tibbets, hurrying toward the trailhead. "My husband was a herpetologist."

"I know," Mr. Lindsey says. "I met him several times. He knew his stuff. "

Tabitha shakes her head and mumbles something to Mrs. Garrett as they try to keep up with the others. Swallows swoop overhead and a mockingbird calls from the branches of a tree in the back field.

"This is an interesting piece of land," Mr. Lindsey says. "There are several different habitats. There's that meadow behind the house, and it looks like there's an outcropping of granite over there."

"And a vernal pool," Ben says hopefully.

The real estate agent swats at the gnats flying around her head.

As they enter the woods, the canopy of leaves above them casts splotchy shadows on the forest floor.

"It's a little wet back here," Mr. Lindsey says. "I don't know if you could build on this part."

"It's always wetter in the spring," the real estate agent says, treading carefully to avoid getting mud on her shiny shoes.

It takes a while for this odd mix of hikers to get through the woods. Mr. Lindsey, Ben, and Mrs. Tibbets stop several times on the path so the two other women can catch up. When they near the vernal pool, Ben runs ahead. It's almost like he wants to warn the pool that people are coming. But when he gets to the big rock, he stops and stares.

There's no pool there.

He can't believe it. It's completely dried up.

If he hadn't seen it with his own eyes, he would never believe there was a pool here only a few days ago. Now it's just a little dip in the ground surrounded by rocks and trees, their leaves casting a deep shadow where the pool had been. Small yellow green bunches of leaves are shooting up out of the spot.

Ben hears the others approaching and turns to face them. "This is the pool," he says, hoping Mr. Lindsey can see something that isn't there. "This is where the spadefoots come."

"But there's nothing here!" exclaims Mrs. Garrett. "Not even a puddle!"

"But it *was* here," Ben says. "It's been here every year. For thousands of years!"

"Oh, really?" says the real estate agent.

Mr. Lindsey squats and looks at the site. They all watch him. He scratches the back of his head, then pushes aside the plants growing up out of the dark, rotting leaves. He presses a finger into the damp earth. He's like a doctor examining a patient.

"What do you think?" Ben asks.

Mr. Lindsey stands up and looks around with his hands on his hips. He steps back several yards, then walks in a circle, checking the ground several times. He scribbles something in the notebook attached to his clipboard. "Well, it could be a significant site," he finally says. "It's a vernal pool for sure."

"But there's nothing here," Mrs. Garrett insists. "Surely you can't say this is a significant site when there's no sign of a pond here."

"Well, yes, ma'am, there are signs. I can tell it's a vernal pool."

Ben smiles and glances over at Mrs. Tibbets. Her eyes are on the place where the pool once was.

"But" —everyone turns to look at Mr. Lindsey—"there are two problems. First, we'd have to document that it contains threatened or endangered species that need vernal pools to survive."

"We saw the spadefoots!" Ben practically shouts. "Mrs. Tibbets has seen them for years."

"Right," says Mr. Lindsey, "but we'd need proof. Pictures or something. It wouldn't have to be spadefoot toads. There are other vernal pool species—fairy shrimp, fingernail clams, and caddisfly larvae, for example. But everything has to be well documented before we can stop any development. "

"Just what I've said all along," says Mrs. Garrett. "You can't hold us up from selling something without proof. I've got a buyer and an owner who is ready to sell. End of story."

"But Mr. Lindsey," Ben begs, "can't you just hold off the builders until we can get the proof?"

"Excuse me, young man!" Mrs. Turner says, really stewing now. "Will you please stay out of this? You have no say here."

"Leave him be, Tabitha!" Mrs. Tibbets snaps. Everybody shuts up and stares at her. "Ben, let Mr. Lindsey talk."

Mr. Lindsey takes off his cap, smooths back his thinning hair, then replaces the cap on his head. "There are other problems. In order to be certified as a vernal pool, the site would have to be filled with water for at least two months. And I'm not sure this pool would be big enough to qualify."

"But that's not fair!" Ben blurts out. "The spadefoots don't care how big it is! They need it to live!"

"Gloria!" Mrs. Turner says to her sister-in-law, glaring at Ben like he's a dog that needs to be disciplined. "Can't you do something about the boy?"

"He's right," Mr. Lindsey says. "It's not fair. But it's the way the laws are written."

"There *are* spadefoot toads here," Mrs. Tibbets says.

"And they *are* endangered," Ben adds.

"I know. I know." Mr. Lindsey tucks his clipboard back

under his arm. "It's a weird little loophole in the law. Spadefoots are particularly difficult to document, since they don't need a very big pool."

"So," the real estate agent says, "it's not really a problem."

Mr. Lindsey looks at her and sighs. "Unless you're a spadefoot."

Ben feels tears welling up in his eyes. He can't believe there's nothing anyone can do. Without another word the adults turn and head back toward the house. Ben falls in beside Mrs. Tibbets, and she places her hand on his shoulder. It's a long, quiet walk. When they reach Mrs. Tibbets's yard, they all stand in the driveway.

Mrs. Garrett breaks the silence. "So, Mr. Lindsey, things have not really changed in terms of what can happen to the land. There's nothing to prevent its sale."

"No..." Mr. Lindsey hesitates. "But you know, if there was real concern about preserving an endangered habitat, it's possible that the sale could be made to a group that would protect it. The Nature Conservancy or the land trust in the town might buy the land. They would pay you and then not develop it."

"But not at its full value," the real estate agent says. "Development is really the way to get the most out of this piece of property. Selling it to some nature group wouldn't be nearly as profitable."

"Not as profitable as putting up a bunch of houses, no."

He looks over at Mrs. Turner. "But I'm sure they would offer a fair price. It's a special piece of land, even if the state can't protect it."

Mrs. Tibbets keeps her eyes on her sister-in-law.

Mrs. Turner stares down at the driveway pavement with a straight mouth, arms folded across her chest. "Thank you, Mr. Lindsey," she says. "We appreciate your time."

Mrs. Tibbets blows a short, exasperated burst of air out of her mouth.

Her sister-in-law frowns. "Selling the land helps you, too, Gloria. Don't make me the bad guy."

It's silent again. Mr. Lindsey takes his wallet out of his pocket and pulls out a card. He hands it to Mrs. Turner. She looks at the card like it's poison, but she takes it.

"If you have any questions or concerns," he says, "give me a call." He shakes hands all around, and comes to Ben last. "It's a pleasure to meet you, young man."

Ben smiles weakly and shakes his hand, but he's hugely disappointed in this man who should have been able to make things right.

As Mr. Lindsey drives away, Mrs. Turner and the real estate woman stand by the van talking quietly.

"I'm going inside, Tabitha," Mrs. Tibbets calls.

"We'll talk later," her sister-in-law answers.

Ben and Mrs. Tibbets watch as the car and the real estate van pull out of the driveway.

"Want a cookie?" Mrs. Tibbets asks, putting a hand on Ben's shoulder.

"Okay," Ben says.

Ben sits at the kitchen table where he's sat a half-dozen times before. The late afternoon sun shines through the window onto Mrs. Tibbets's hands, resting on the table just across from him.

It's over, Ben thinks. *All of this, and nothing happens. The houses get built. The spadefoots lose their home.* "Isn't there anything you can say to your sister-in-law?" he asks.

Mrs. Tibbets shakes her head. "There's not a thing I can do. We're just too far apart, and she wouldn't listen to me no matter what I said."

"But Mr. Lindsey said she could still make money even if she sold the land to people who would take care of it."

"I know. But she's got her mind made up. They have a buyer who's willing to pay a lot of money. I can't imagine what would make her change her mind."

Ben looks out the window and tries to picture the trees gone and the land filled up with houses. "Your husband wouldn't have sold the land so someone could build houses on it, would he?"

"No, he loved this land."

"Doesn't she love it too?"

"You'd think so—she grew up on it. I tried reminding her of that, but she wouldn't listen. She won't listen to anything I say."

Some of Mrs. Tibbets's words catch Ben's attention. *She grew up on it.* An idea hits him.

"Mrs. Tibbets, where are those pictures?"

"What pictures?"

"You know, those old pictures you were going through a couple of weeks ago? Where are they?"

"On the dining room table."

Ben jumps up and runs to the dining room. He brings the box back into the kitchen and dumps the contents onto the table. Mrs. Tibbets watches him without speaking as he searches through the yellowed old photographs.

He finds the snapshot he's looking for and holds it up in the fading daylight. It's the picture of the two kids sitting on the rock. Suddenly he realizes that it's the rock he and Mrs. Tibbets sat on by the vernal pool. He gazes at the picture, watching the years fall away. The girl is Tabitha and the boy is Thomas. They are both holding American toads. The girl has a big grin and doesn't look anything like the grown-up Mrs. Tabitha Turner.

Ben flips over the photo. Scrawled on the back are these words: *Tom, me, and the Overtoad.* He turns over the picture again and looks at the girl holding the toad. The Overtoad.

Tabitha and the Overtoad. "Mrs. Tibbets, this *is* Tabitha, isn't it?"

Mrs. Tibbets takes the photo and holds it at arm's length. "Yes," she says, squinting. "It's Tabitha and Thomas."

"Look at what she wrote on the back. She knows about the Overtoad!"

"You mean she *knew* about it. When she was little."

"But she forgot," Ben says.

"Yes, she forgot. Things happen when you grow up. And you forget."

Mrs. Tibbets gets up to put the dishes in the sink, and Ben slips the photo into his jacket pocket. "I have to go now," he says. "I need to get to work on my geography report."

Mrs. Tibbets dries her hands on a dish towel. "Your report? I thought you said it was due today."

"It was, but Mrs. Kutcher gave me another week. I changed what I'm doing it on. If I don't finish it this time, she'll kill me."

"I doubt that."

"Well, bye," Ben says and scoots out the back door. There's so much to do, and he doesn't know if he has enough time. But he whirls around and sticks his head back through the doorway. "Mrs. Tibbets, maybe the Overtoad will save us."

"I would love that," Mrs. Tibbets says.

Two days later, on a hot Sunday afternoon, Ben leads Ryan and Jenny down the path from his house. They're all carrying supplies for the expedition, and Jenny's got her camera slung around her neck. Ryan drops the plastic containers he's carrying, and they skitter across the trail. Ben and Jenny help him pick them up.

"It's good your body parts are attached," Jenny says, "or you'd lose them, too."

Ryan laughs. "Like you never lose anything! You're so perfect!"

Jenny smiles.

Ben slows down to check his pocket. Did he forget the list of things to search for at the site of the vernal pool? No, it's still there, along with the pictures he printed from the Internet.

—eggs from fairy shrimp

—caddisfly cases

—snail shells

—fingernail clams

Nothing they're looking for is longer than two inches. But Ben hopes he can find some specimens to show what lives in a vernal pool. He wants to show everything he can in his report.

When they get to the site of the pool, Ben stops. "Here it is," he says.

Ryan and Jenny stare at the mud-encrusted, leaf-strewn ground.

"I don't see any pool," says Ryan.

"I told you. That's what a vernal pool does," says Ben. "It dries up."

"But there's nothing left to find!" Ryan says.

"There's got to be something. Help me look. And Jenny, will you take some pictures of the area?"

Ben steps carefully out to the middle of the darkened leaves where the pool was and squats down.

Ryan starts shoving leaves and dirt aside. "I don't see anything!" he says.

"Hey!" Ben yells. "You've got to be more careful. We don't want to mess everything up."

While Jenny snaps pictures, Ryan and Ben work quietly and methodically, sifting through the mud. First Ben finds a caddisfly casing. Then Ryan shouts, "Hey, look! A little clamshell! And here's another one!"

"I know," Ben says. "It's like there's nothing there, but then you look closely and *bam!* a whole different world opens up!"

Within fifteen minutes they fill a couple of containers with snails, clams, and caddisfly shells.

"Too bad we can't get a spadefoot," says Ryan.

"They're around here somewhere," says Ben. "But they're impossible to find." Just then something moves in the leaves by his feet. He bends over and pushes the leaves aside. Ben gently places his hand over the creature and picks it up.

"Is it a spadefoot?" Ryan asks.

"Nope," says Ben. "It's a wood frog. Remember the one I brought into school? They use vernal pools, too." He opens his hand carefully. "Look at it!" The three of them peer down at its tan, smooth skin and the dark mask around its eyes.

"It's cool!" Ryan says.

Ben looks at the frog. Then he looks at Jenny and Ryan. An idea comes into his head. A great idea.

"You guys, go sit on that rock over there," Ben says, pointing to the boulder by the side of the pool.

"How come?" Ryan asks.

"Just do it, please!"

Jenny shakes her head, but she follows Ryan to the rock and clambers up behind him.

"Um, Jenny, can I use your camera?" Ben asks. He takes the camera from her and puts the strap around his neck. "One more thing," he says, handing the frog to Jenny. "You have to hold this. Hold it up so I can see it."

"No way. What if it poops on me?"

"Consider yourself blessed. Just take it. I'll hurry."

They're laughing as Ben focuses the camera on them. "Okay," he says. "Jenny, hold the frog a little higher. Both of you guys smile."

"Ribbet," Ryan says. *"Ribbet, ribbet, ribbet."*

Ben clicks the picture.

Ben works like crazy on the report. For the next five days, it's all he thinks about.

The best part about a report is what it feels like when it's finished. It's like Ben hasn't taken a deep breath for weeks, and suddenly his lungs are filled with fresh air. Or like he's taken off a pair of really dark sunglasses and can finally see clearly again.

And when he's finished he knows it's good. He just hopes it's good enough.

It's raining, but by the time Ben finds the street he's looking for, it has started to pour. He's drenched, but his report is inside his jacket, safely tucked into a plastic bag. He pedals his bike slowly so he can see the street numbers, then he recognizes the car in one of the driveways. Ben parks his bike on the sidewalk, walks to the door, and knocks. Nobody answers, so he knocks again. He's about to give up when the door opens.

Tabitha Turner stands there looking surprised. "Yes?"

"Hello, Mrs. Turner. I'm Ben Moroney." Drops of rain trickle from his hair and slide down his nose. He wipes his face with the sleeve of his jacket. "I met you at Mrs. Tibbets's house."

"I know who you are."

"I'm really sorry to bother you, but I've got something I want to show you. It's my report for geography."

She raises one eyebrow. "Geography?"

"Yes, ma'am. Geography. It'll just take a minute. Please?"

Tabitha Turner looks back in the house like she's trying to figure out a way to escape, but she steps to the side and motions for Ben to come in. "You can hang your wet jacket on that coat rack," she tells him. "And maybe you'd better leave your shoes by the door."

Ben does as he's told and follows Mrs. Turner into a large living room. She sits in a straight-backed chair by the window. Ben checks the seat of his jeans to make sure it isn't wet, then perches on the edge of the couch. With his heart pounding, he slides his report out of the plastic bag and places it on the coffee table.

"I wanted to show you my report on ecosystems," he says, scooting it over so she can see it.

She glances down at the report, then looks at him blankly, like she's still trying to figure out what he's talking about.

"Um, I was going to do it on the desert, because that's where I lived until four months ago. I really loved it there. There was this great museum near my house, and I had all this stuff about deserts. I even had a lizard—its name was Lenny—but I didn't get to bring it with me when I moved. My friend Toby was keeping it and it died."

Mrs. Turner nods, waiting to hear what this is all about.

"But when I started my desert report, I didn't feel like doing it anymore." Ben is halfway afraid to go on, but there's nothing to do but just plow ahead.

"So instead I decided to do it about what it's like where I live now." He takes a deep breath and lets it out. "I decided to do it about your land. About your vernal pool."

Tabitha Turner clears her throat and shifts uncomfortably in her chair as if she's about to speak, but Ben doesn't give her a chance to interrupt. He opens his report and holds it out to her.

"I know you don't have time to read all of this, but here I talk about how the pool has been there a really long time—probably for ten thousand years. And about the people who have lived there. The Wampanoag Indians walked through here maybe a thousand years ago. They were the ones who met the Pilgrims."

Ben thumbs through until he finds the photos. "See, here are some of the animals that live in vernal pools. These are salamanders—spotted ones, I'm pretty sure. We didn't find any in your pool, but they live around here. And look at these caddisfly larvae. They make these little buildings out of sticks." He holds the booklet up so she can see the little clamshells he taped to the sheet. "I found these at the pool site. And I figure there were fairy shrimp, too, but I couldn't find any. I know spadefoots were there earlier this spring, but they're all spread out now. Still, me and my friends did find something interesting."

Ben flips to the last page, where he's taped the picture of Ryan and Jenny sitting on the big rock by the dried-up pool. They're both laughing, and Jenny's nose is scrunched up. She's holding the wood frog away from her because she's afraid it's going to poop on her.

Ben has barely looked at Mrs. Turner the whole time. But now he sneaks a glance. She's studying the picture of Ryan and Jenny. There is the barest hint of a smile on her face. He wonders if she knows. He's about to find out. He barrels ahead with what he's been planning to say. What could happen here is more important than any grade he's going to get in geography.

"And I put that picture at the end of the report because of the picture I put at the front of it."

Ben flips back to the first page of the report and holds it up for Tabitha Turner to see.

The picture is old and crinkled on the edges. It shows two kids sitting on a rock, holding toads. The girl is holding the fat toad under her chin and laughing.

Tabitha Turner's breath catches. Ben looks up at her and sees her hand go to her mouth. But he's not done.

"Let me read the first page," he says. Ben reads aloud, over the sound of his heart pounding in his chest. "There is a habitat close to me that I just discovered. It's like another planet. Even though it's small, it holds a thousand things. And once there were these two kids who lived near it. They were brother and sister. They made up a funny story about a giant spirit that looked after the land. They called the creature the Overtoad. This is the story of the land and water that the Overtoad protects. It has protected it for thousands of years, and I hope it protects it for thousands more. My report is about a vernal pool in Edenboro, Massachusetts."

Ben watches as Tabitha Turner takes her hand from her mouth and reaches out for the report. He hands it to her. After staring at the picture for a moment, she looks at the ceiling like she's trying to see right through it to the sky, then closes the report. She opens it again and leafs through the booklet page by page. When she gets to the picture of Ryan and Jenny, she stares at it, then flips back to the picture of her and her brother.

"Mrs. Turner," Ben pleads. "Please don't let them put up the houses where the toads are. I know it's your land. But please don't do it. Mrs. Tibbets doesn't want you do it, either, but she thinks you're mad at her. I know you don't get along. She says you won't listen to her."

Tabitha Turner gives him a sad smile. "I know what my sister-in-law thinks," she says. She pauses for a moment, then asks, "Does she know you're doing this?"

Ben shakes his head. "She thinks it's too late. I was hoping you might sell it to somebody who won't put houses on it, but she says you won't change your mind."

He looks at Tabitha Turner. Her face shows nothing. Suddenly Ben is exhausted. He never should have done this. Mrs. Tibbets was right.

Mrs. Turner stands, the report still in her hands.

"Um...I'll need that back," Ben says.

"What will you do with the picture?" she asks, handing him the booklet.

"I'll give it back to Mrs. Tibbets."

"If it's all right, I'd like it," Tabitha Turner says.

"Okay," Ben says. "When I get the report back, I'll ask her if I can give it to you."

"Actually," she adds, "I'd like both of them. The other one, too."

"Sure," Ben says. "Okay."

Mrs. Turner leads him to the front door and opens it. "Thank you for coming by, Ben," she says.

"Okay," Ben says, "If you want—"

"You don't need to say anything more," she says. "Thanks for coming by."

Ben climbs on his bike for the long ride home. When he looks back, Mrs. Turner is standing behind the storm door watching him. He feels empty.

It's all up to the Overtoad now.

The next day, when Ben sets his terrarium and his report on the big table at the back of the classroom, a bunch of kids gathers around.

"What's in there?" someone asks.

"Wetland plants," Ben says.

"Any snakes?" Danny Martin asks.

Ben shakes his head.

"Toads?" someone else asks. "Frogs?"

"There's an American toad in there," Ben says.

"I can't see it," Danny says.

"It's camouflaged," Ben says. "It doesn't want you to see it."

"Let's take it out," another kid says.

"I think we should leave it alone," Ben says. "It's already freaked out about where it is. I'm going to take it back to the woods tomorrow."

"Why don't you keep it?" Tommy Miller asks.

"I don't feel like it," says Ben. His classmates try to find the toad in the terrarium, but lose interest after a while and drift back to their desks. That's when Ben notices Jenny leafing through his report.

"Jeez, Ben, this is really long!" she says.

"I know," Ben says, "I kind of got carried away."

Ryan appears at Jenny's side. "Let me see!" he says and grabs for it. "Whoa, it's a million pages."

"Fifteen, actually," Jenny says.

"Almost a million," Ryan says, flipping the pages.

"Don't mess it up," says Ben, "or I'll feed you to the Overtoad." As he says that, Mrs. Kutcher comes up behind Ben.

"Did you bring this in, Ben?" she says, looking down at the terrarium.

"Yeah," he says. "It's part of my report." He takes the report out of Ryan's hands and gives it to Mrs. Kutcher. She thumbs through it, and a huge smile spreads across her face.

"Great work, Ben! Great, great work!"

Ben grins. It *is* great work and he knows it.

Chapter Eighteen

After school on Wednesday Ben's heading into the kitchen for his snack when the phone rings. He grabs the receiver before his sister can get there.

"No fair," she says. "You always get it first."

He holds his hand over the mouthpiece for a second. "So? Life's not fair."

"I hate it when you say that!" Agatha shouts. She dashes out the back door and slams it behind her.

Ben turns back to the phone. Someone is chuckling. "Ben?" a voice says.

"Yes?"

"It's Mrs. Tibbets. Is your mother there? I'd like to speak to her."

Ben hesitates. "Um...okay."

"It's nothing bad, Ben. I just need to talk with her for a minute."

Ben hands the receiver to his mom, who says hi to Mrs. Tibbets. He doesn't know what to make of it when, after a minute of listening, she starts laughing. "I see," she says, looking over at Ben. "All right." She hangs up and announces, "Mrs. Tibbets is picking you up in about fifteen minutes."

"For what?"

"She'll tell you."

"But Mom!"

"I'm sorry, you'll just have to wait."

Ben tries to wheedle it out of her, but when he sees it's no use he goes outside to wait. A long half hour later, Mrs. Tibbets's station wagon pulls into the driveway. She leans over and opens the door.

"Hi!" Ben says as he hops in.

"Hello, Ben." Mrs. Tibbets backs out of the driveway and heads down the street.

Ben waits for her to say something, but she keeps her eyes on the road and her mouth shut. "Where are we going?" he finally asks.

"To my house," she says.

When they round the last corner, Ben sees Tabitha Turner standing beside her car in the driveway. Someone Ben hasn't seen before is next to her.

"Hello, Ben," Mrs. Turner says as he and Mrs. Tibbets get out of the car.

"Hi," he says. He looks from person to person, trying to get a sense of what this is all about.

"I asked Gloria if she thought you'd like to come over. We've just been talking to Mr. Selby here. He's with the local land trust."

Ben opens his mouth, then closes it again. No one says anything for a minute—they're all looking at each other, trying to figure out who should speak first.

"I've decided to sell most of the property to the land trust," Tabitha finally says. "I'm holding on to a two-acre plot on the other side of the vernal pool, where we may put up a few houses."

Ben nods, still too stunned to speak.

"The spadefoots will be all right. I thought you should know."

Ben looks at Mrs. Tibbets, then back at Mrs. Turner. "You changed your mind," Ben says.

Mrs. Turner nods her head. "Yes. Someone made me change my mind."

Ben's face breaks into a huge grin. "That's great. That's really great," he says. "Thanks. Thank you so much."

"You're welcome," Mrs. Turner says.

"No, I mean really thanks."

"And I mean you're really welcome." Mrs. Turner gets in her car, starts the motor, then rolls down the window. "One more thing, Ben. If you see the Overtoad, thank her for me."

"Okay," says Ben.

"Maybe someone should name the trail by the pool the Overtoad Trail," Mrs. Tibbets says.

Mrs. Turner looks at her sister-in-law and manages a smile. "That's a good idea," she says. The land trust man shakes Mrs. Tibbets's hand and gets in the passenger side of Mrs. Turner's car. Ben and Mrs. Tibbets wave as the car pulls away.

Without a word, like they speak the same silent language, Mrs. Tibbets and Ben walk around the garage and head toward the woods. Ben feels his feet connect with the ground like he's part of it and it's part of him. As they enter the trees a breeze pushes the branches back and forth, showing the silvery undersides of the leaves. They come closer and closer to the place where the vernal pool was—and will be again. Suddenly Mrs. Tibbets draws in a breath and stops.

"Ohmigosh!" she whispers, holding an arm out in front of Ben.

"What is it?" he whispers.

"Look. Just look!" She points to the path ahead. Ben looks where she's pointing and the hair rises on his arms.

It's a rattlesnake, crossing the path about ten feet in front of them, sliding quietly over the dirt and leaves. Another one follows it. Ben and Mrs. Tibbets watch them until they disappear into the undergrowth.

"I don't believe it," Mrs. Tibbets murmurs. "I just don't believe it."

They both stand there for a moment, barely breathing. They're surrounded by the small sounds of the woods. Far off in the distance they can hear a car motor.

Finally Mrs. Tibbets breaks the silence. "Well," she says. "I guess we're just going to have to be a little more careful around here from now on. It seems that we have some new neighbors."

"I hope they feel at home," Ben says.

"I hope you do, too, Ben," Mrs. Tibbets says.

"I do," he says.

And he does. Right at home.

The End

Author's Note

Resources for Toad Lovers and Vernal Pool Savers

Saving the rain forests is important, but don't forget about your own neighborhood. Vernal pools don't look like much, but they harbor species like the spadefoot toad that are an important part of the web of life. They need our protection, too, and they're right around the corner, if we take the time to look. Many students around the United States have worked to save vernal pools in their areas. You can, too!

To learn more about vernal pools, check out these resources.

In print

The Frog Book, by Mary Dickerson (Dover). An old but accurate and beautifully written book about all the species of frogs found in the U.S. It's a classic.

Frog Heaven: Ecology of a Vernal Pool, by Doug Wechsler (Boyds). A great book, especially for students.

Last Child in the Woods, by Richard Louv (Algonquin Books). A book about the importance of nature in children's lives.

Vernal Pool Lessons and Activities, by Nancy Childs and Betsy Colburn, and *Certified: A Citizen's Step-by-Step Guide to Protecting Vernal Pools,* Elizabeth A. Colburn, ed. (Massachusetts Audubon Society). An excellent workbook and a useful field manual for young people and teachers interested in identifying and preserving vernal pools and the critters that thrive in them.

Vernal Pools: Natural History and Conservation, by Betsy Colburn (MacDonald and Woodward). Everything you ever wondered about when it comes to vernal pools.

On the web

A search for "vernal pools" or "spadefoot toads" will turn up a wealth of information. And don't forget to look on YouTube and other video sites for some great videos of kids and adults working to save vernal pools.

Some websites you might like to consult:

http://www.vernalpool.org
The Vernal Pool Association offers resources for students and community people who want to identify and preserve vernal pools.

www.sacsplash.org/mather.htm
An informative video about vernal pools.

You can also contact your local nature center or state department of natural resources for more information about vernal pools, amphibians, and other critters in the wild—and in your backyard!